The Queen of Evil

Romance

The Queen of Evil

Abdenal Carvalho

SUMMARY

Prologue

After I was freed from the curse of being the wife of the Evil One and living for several centuries at his service, becoming known in the world of mortals as Pomba-Gira, the Queen of prostitutes, influencing sexual immorality in alienated humanity from her Creator, I reincarnated on earth again in the figure of a woman inclined to live in chastity.

At the age of fifteen, due to my extreme vocation for the poorest and the enormous inclination to religiosity, my parents placed me in a convent, where from then on I would become one of the nuns best known throughout Europe for the profound mercy that moved me towards the social classes most wronged by hunger and misery.

There were several persecutions suffered throughout the journey, criticism, mockery, humiliation of all sorts, but I remained firm in the decision to never give up the choice made the day I first wore that garment and swore total dedication to the church in the mission of evangelize, care, heal wounds, always be ready to extend my hands to those who by God's designs cross my path.

My baptismal name was Tereza, I was born on August 26, 1910 in Albania, from an early age I dedicated myself to religious life on behalf of the poor and since then I have accomplished great things for them in the name of God and the church, however a great disappointment waited.

First Chapter: Divine Rejection

That cold winter morning I was taken from my body after living for almost a century among mortals in the physical form of a woman who, unlike the previous incarnation, never let herself be contaminated with the sin of sexual immorality nor allowed her to take away the purity brought with it from birth, I remained chaste until death.

From my spiritual counselors I learned early that the children of Mary, mother of God, behave in holiness through chastity, where we deny the sexual act that contaminates the purity of the human soul, I have never even been touched or kissed by anyone, except my own. parents, when he still lived alongside them.

Due to my life dedicated to mercy towards the most needy, due to the way I remained captive to divine precepts from a young age, avoiding the sin of lust, lust and everything that would separate me from the intimate relationship with the Holy Church, I seriously believed that he would have a special place waiting for me in his Kingdom, however, I was wrong.

While a large crowd of people surrounded the coffin where my body rested from the daily drudgery, lived for nine decades, on a plane parallel to human reality I saw everything without being noticed. Suddenly everything became clear to me, because when the spirit disincarnates it remembers everything that it lived in its past lives, it is as if it were a movie in repetition before your eyes.

I remembered Michael, the Archangel who, along with thousands of other warriors, descended to the lower parts of the earth just to rescue me from the prisons of hell. The forgiveness received from the Eternal Father, the opportunity to atone for my guilt for having stood by the Demo for several centuries, encouraging humanity to commit illicit and shameful acts that led many to eternal condemnation. I therefore had the opportunity to return to this world to suffer for the poorest.

However, to my disappointment, upon arriving in the presence of the Most High I was not received with the expected honors, as I was accused of practicing the sin of idolatry during all my days of existence on earth. An audience with the Almighty was already prepared for me, which would define the sentence for my case.

The angel who was in charge of coming to pick me up after disincarnating said nothing about it, just took me to the Celestial Mansions where they awaited my return so that I would be held responsible for the acts practiced while I was alive. A court was formed by God the Father, God the Son, and his Holy Spirit, both of whom proceeded to bring the appropriate charges.

— Do you understand the reasons for this Divine Jury to meet to find you guilty according to your actions while living in the world of mortals? Are you aware of your disobedience to the divine precepts demanded by the Lord Almighty?

— I am grateful that I am allowed to speak in this judgment. Yes, I understand that according to the charges presented I deserve to be present in this court to account for my alleged acts of disobedience.

However, I do not agree with such accusation.

— And why do you disagree with the performance of this Council?

— For almost a century I was entirely dedicated to a life of piety and mercy towards the poorest, I gave up freedom of choice and chose to faithfully serve charity towards my fellow men in total obedience to the dictates of the church. So, explain to me why I am being found guilty of mistakes I never made before?

— When you were rescued from the slavery of sexual sin, together with servitude to the greatest enemy of this Kingdom, you received from the Eternal Father the opportunity to return to the earth and reincarnate there for a new beginning.

We understand that in fact you chose a living caste, giving up his free will, you remained pure physically and spiritually, you fulfilled the second greatest commandment of the Gospel which is to love your neighbor as yourself, but you have committed the worst of all human errors, the idolatry.

You disobeyed the first and most important of all the commandments of the Law of the Lord by serving, worshiping, worshiping and worshiping a sculpture image made by the hands of men. This was your biggest sin!

— From an early age I learned that Mary was the mother of God and that she should be worshiped, since the Scriptures affirmed that she was the greatest and most important among all women, so I believed in this teaching, I turned that doctrine of the church into truth, fulfilling it with all the strength of my heart, deviating neither to the right nor to the left

— In fact we are aware of this…

Because as you well know we have the power to make us present everywhere at the same time and to know all things, but his dedication and fidelity was not to this Kingdom nor to the God of the entire Universe who he sits on his throne above the clouds, placing himself above all things. He alone should be given all honor, all praise, all worship. For this reason this Council finds you guilty of transgression against the Sacred Laws, condemning you to a new reincarnation on earth for the atonement of this terrible sin!

After the sentence was applied against me without being given the possibility of a new defense in my favor, I was led by the angel to a certain part of the Kingdom, where souls separated to reincarnate on earth were properly prepared, then sent to their new destination. It turns out that from that moment on I would feel wronged.

I would take with me the bitter revolt of not being recognized before my God for the immense dedication to the humanitarian cause, the love of neighbor, the practice of charity, the chastity that did not allow me to love and be loved, to marry, to have children and to have a family. All that lack of consideration for sacrifices made in the name of faith and the church left me upset.

In seconds everything was erased, I went from a spiritual reality to a deep sleep that seems to have lasted for many days, weeks and months. I woke up in a cold dawn when being pulled out of my mother's womb, with a strong spanking on the buttocks given by the midwife who performed the birth, it was there that I made my life and started a new journey in yet another story written by the evil owner of the destiny human.

Second Chapter: Revenge

I was born on a cold Saturday where the roofs of the houses, trees and streets were covered by heavy snow that fell all night before, it was a winter in which no clothes are able to contain, taking those who do not have an airy place to living end up losing their lives in the gutters of misery. My new Christian name was Luana.

My father was a tall, strong man, with reddish skin, on his face there was, besides a well-shaved beard, an air of intense happiness with my arrival, his name was Paulo. My mother was strong, she resisted everything very willingly, she did not give up the pain felt during that home birth and without many medical resources, she was called Maria.

However, this was not assimilated by me who had barely arrived in that place, my mind still empty could not understand anything perfectly, this is the most difficult part of a reincarnation. Because we receive a new body, whose mind is empty as a blank paper, the reality around us becomes embarrassing, meaningless.

During my first years of life I was treated like a princess by my parents, uncles and the rest of the family, I was the first granddaughter, the pride of my grandparents, I also had the privilege of being an only child. My parents were very hardworking, wanting to give me the best and the best. But they were poor and uneducated, this led me to want to provide them with a better existence.

To free them from that miserable condition in which my father had to leave the house at dawn in search of work or some other way of keeping the family, returning only in the early evening, often empty-handed and without hope. Of course, I started to understand these things and think of a way to help them only from nine to ten years old, when the reason for what woke me up came to light, to realize that our life was not made of chocolate. Thankfully, Mom had uterine complications which prevented her from having other children, this helped a lot to avoid further unnecessary expenses.

After completing my ten years of age I chose to study in the morning and take care of a rich child in the afternoon, initially Dad was opposed, he did not want to see his princess in that situation, served as a "black girl" for the children of the barons, my mother ended up convince him of the enormous need that we had to raise more money.

My trip to the Dantas' house, the richest family in the city, was the first mistake I made in the drug of another existence in this world where poor human beings never get it right. At that age, I understood nothing about life or the risks of being born a beautiful woman from an early age, I was physically perfect.

My body developed with amazing speed, even without reaching puberty, I already had a guitar waist and pairs of thighs to cause envy in many teenagers older than me, without taking into account the fleshy and upturned butt that I inherited from mom. The boys drooled all the time. Hence the fact that I mentioned earlier that going to work as a nanny at the Dantas millionaire residence would have been a mistake.

14

That family was formed by the couple, a three-year-old child and their two playboy children, the type who, because they are rich, think they own the world, abusing people without showing any respect for them. They were two unscrupulous teenagers who did what they wanted, they all got ready without having to give an account for any of their mistakes. The youngest was the worst of all, he did not even listen to his parents' demands, stubborn and foolish. At fourteen, he refused to have any form of responsibility.

His name was Pedro, irresistibly handsome in spite of his bad character, he was the one who first approached me with the worst intentions, even though until that time of events due to my excessive naivete I did not realize his real purposes for me, a country hick , daughter of two poor people without any social values.

Exactly for belonging to a poor family, without the least financial resources, the bastard understood that he could abuse me without my parents being able to demand any form of reparation for the evil that he might do to me, because he had the habit of acting in this way with the daughters of many others who lived on the periphery.

It turns out that that brat stepped on the ball, arranging a huge mess for his life and that of his parents, but that I explain in another part of this account, for now we will follow every detail of the facts experienced by mm in my last incarnation. In the first month of my stay at the mansion I was approached by the pervert. It was a morning on one of those days when the mansion's employees were busy with their household chores and I absentmindedly took care of the family's youngest son, when I was suddenly approached by the teenager who gave me a strong hug from behind.

Letting him touch my upturned butt something hard, looking like a sword. The correct thing would be for me to scream for help, to try to free myself from his clutches, but my attitude was passive and as soon as the surprise of not knowing who it was was gone, I was calm, letting him kiss my neck under the long curly hair, rubbing his huge mast on my buttocks, everything seemed natural to me, it was as if I expected that.

In fact, since I got there, I noticed that kid's hungry look in my direction, eating my ass and thighs with his eyes, I had even gotten used to his strange attitude. When I didn't see him hanging around the house, I missed him, everything seemed boring, even though I was just a child at that time I fell in love.

Now imagine the madness, what would the relationship between a poor girl and the son of a millionaire end? Undoubtedly the end would be disastrous. The touch of his body next to mine excited me, raised my hair from the legs to the head, it was a real madness that I loved feeling, it was a new experience that fascinated me.

The correct thing is that a woman only feels sexual desires after reaching puberty, but with me it happened differently, I was just touched by the opposite sex and I felt the pulse of immense almost irresistible pleasure burning inside me. At that first moment Pedro turned me around, grabbed my mouth, sticking his warm, soft tongue inside it.

Then he sucked on mine, making me feel that delicious shiver down my spine again and driving me crazy. While he kissed me, even without the height, his hands explored my body, caressed my breasts, the belly, the private parts. All that madness made me burn, shiver.

That naive but hardworking and struggling girl, from that moment on, would feel a profound change in her feelings to the point of allowing her crazy naivete to lead her to make irreparable mistakes that would compromise not only her own life, but that of everyone she loved, because they would act against their oppressors.

We spent two years dating their parents' hideouts, as they would in no way agree to our union. Pedro and I looked like a couple of teenagers in love, but deep down I was the one who had given my heart to the bastard in addition to everything else. At the age of twelve, he at eighteen, we lay down again and the worst happened.

My body matured faster than I expected, I became a woman instantly, the first menstrual rule came and I got pregnant in our last sex. Since I did not fully understand the symptoms of pregnancy, the constant nausea tormented me for weeks, drawing the attention of the other employees, who immediately told their bosses.

— Madam, I think that the girl Luana is ill, lives with constant vomiting

— Then call Dr. Daniel to see you, Marta

— Okay, ma'am, I'll do it right away!

Marta was the housekeeper of the Dantas mansion, responsible for managing all the other employees, very energetic and observant, nothing went by without her being observed. When I heard about the doctor's coming to assess my health condition, I was very excited, because I wanted to be cured, I never imagined that the situation I found myself in was different.

— Luana, take a decent shower, get dressed and wait for the doctor to arrive for an appointment!

— Yes ma'am...

As soon as the doctor arrived they took him to a large office where he usually consulted all employees on a monthly basis to see if everything was going well with them, as our bosses were afraid that any type of disease would be transmitted to their children, which I thought was quite fair. That afternoon on a beautiful Friday my secret would be revealed.

After carefully evaluating me, Dr. Daniel talked privately with the housekeeper, who ordered me to collect some urine, blood and feces to be taken to a laboratory for routine examination, from a more serious face than usual, I realized that the conversation with the doctor it hadn't been very pleasant, so I shivered with fear.

I wondered what the doctor's diagnosis would have been after examining me, would I have a contagious disease, would I die in a few days or be dismissed from work? The salary paid to me by Dantas wasn't much, but it was helping a lot in my family's budget and my parents were managing to lead a more peaceful life, losing my job at that moment would be terrible.

I soon found myself completely concerned with the situation in which I found myself, as I was not sure what awaited me from that moment on. The material requested by the housekeeper was delivered and for two distressing days I waited for the result that would come from the laboratory of clinical analyzes, my heart pounded non-stop. The forty-eight hours of waiting were the longest I've ever lived in my life, until they finally came to an end.

Marta received an envelope that afternoon, containing detailed information about my state of health, after reading she scratched her head covered by her gray hair and went to meet Ms. Emília Dantas, the boss.

— Madam, here's the result of Luana's exams done in the laboratory

— Then you should hand them over to Dr. Daniel for him to assess the girl's situation, Marta, you know how it works, he determines which treatment and you perform

— Sorry missus, but I was too curious and took a look at the results

— You're losing track of things, woman, don't you know that opening a sealed envelope without belonging to you is a crime? This information was directed only to the doctor, you shouldn't have done such a thing!

— I know that, ma'am, but I think that after reading what you say here you will understand the reasons for my behavior

The mistress received the envelope from the maid's hands, read the information related to my urine test and turned yellow.

— Oh my God!

— Yes, missus, I had already suspected because of the symptoms presented in the girl and I did not refrain from curiosities

— But who could have done such a barbarity with this poor girl on my property? Was it one of our employees? We need to investigate this immediately, Marta, I want this monster to be identified.

And punished for what it did!

— Yes, ma'am, I will take the necessary measures!

Immediately, as the mistress had ordered, all male employees who worked at the mansion were asked to appear before the housekeeper in a large meeting room and were questioned as to what had happened in order to identify the rapist, however, all those present said innocent.

Being a powerful woman because of the immense wealth that Mrs. Dantas possessed, she decided to take an exam in a clinic specialized in rape with me and all the men who worked on her property in order to identify the rapist, as she did not accept the evil that had befallen her. me right inside his house, he didn't even know his son was to blame.

Until that moment, nothing was told to me about what was happening, I saw the uproar, people walking around, employees being tested, meetings, but nothing was said about it. They only ordered me to stay in my rooms, someone else took care of the child, so I saw that I really lost my job. However, two days later I was asked to appear before my employer.

— Sit down, Luana, we need to have a very serious conversation

— Yes ma'am...

— You have lived with us in this house for two years and we are very grateful for the way you have taken care of our youngest son during all this time, since it is possible to observe his intense zeal and dedication in caring for him. However, something very serious happened to you here inside this house that needs to be clarified and the culprit punished for such evil, I called you to come here so that you can tell us who the monster was that did such a thing!

I confess that when I heard it I shut up without knowing what to say.

Did she find out that Pedro and I had sex? But was it possible? I didn't get an answer when making so many speculations for myself, so I decided to argue in an ironic way, trying to disguise the truth that I knew very well."But, madam, what evil do you mean?"

— Don't be naive, girl, we are already aware of everything that happened to you, tell us right away who was the monster that dared to rape you so that we can do due justice in your favor!

Oh my God, our secret has been discovered, what will become of me and Pedro? — I thought in despair — I could not reveal that he was the author of that thoughtless act, because it would be a terrible disappointment for his parents, besides that he loved him above my strength and would never want to harm him. The solution was to deny everything, to pretend to be so innocent to the point of not even knowing how he had lost his virginity and see what happened.

— Sorry, ma'am, but I still can't understand the meaning of this conversation or your words

— Oh no? Who are you trying to cover up, girl, do you happen to think we are so stupid as to believe that you slept and woke up pregnant? That revelation fell like a bomb on my head, I immediately changed my mind about denying what happened or keeping secret about who would have been the author of that act that led me to bear his child inside my womb, after all, Pedro would have to assume his responsibilities towards me.

So, I decided to open the game in front of Marta and our boss.

— Good heavens, girl, are you okay? — The housekeeper was concerned

— Get her some sugar water, Marta, she looks very shaken!

After a few minutes I felt better again, because knowing that at that age I would be pregnant disturbed me a lot, I thought that the issue there was just the fact that I was no longer a virgin, however, the situation was much worse than I imagined. What would you say to my parents? How would Dad react to a revelation like that, with me being his only daughter?

He always saw me as his little princess, his treasure, he had an incomparable zeal for me and nothing in this world would prevent him from punishing anyone who did me any harm. But it's okay — I thought to myself — certainly the boss will not want to see her blood poured into the gutter, her first grandson would have special treatment, no doubt she would demand a marriage to match. Pedro was old enough to assume his responsibilities. Thinking this way, I calmed down and decided to reveal everything in the smallest detail to the two women who were sitting right in front of me:

— Well, then if my situation is this I will tell you exactly what happened. As soon as I arrived at the mansion, I was besieged by the young Pedro who started to make declarations of love to me, kissing me in the moments when I was distracted. With that I became attached to him and ended up giving in to his charms, allowing him to possess me

— There are two people with the same name on this property, girl, which one do you refer to?

— Your son, lady

— Did my Pedro commit this insanity?

No, I refuse to believe it, you can only want to throw this blame on my boy to get along!

— No, missus, I swear that's not true!

— How could a girl of only ten years have fallen in love with a boy of sixteen? How did you feel desires to the point of having sex with him if you hadn't even really become a woman? — Asked the housekeeper

— Exactly, explain to us how this could happen if it was just a child who at that age is only interested in playing with her dolls?

— I do not know, as the ladies can perceive I am a different girl from the others, although very young my body developed quickly, I have the appearance of being older than I really have.

Pedro realized this and insisted that I have sex with him, at first I refused completely, but a huge desire took over me every time he hugged me, during our kisses, his touch caused me to shiver from head to toe

— Please stop describing your moments of intimacy with my son, if you are really telling us the truth!

— Can you believe so, ma'am, I have no reason to lie

— Well, it will be your word against his, we will put them face to face and if he confirms what he has just told us we will take the necessary measures to solve this problem, but if his answer is contrary to what he told us to be no more stay in this house, come back to live with your parents and never put your feet here again, understand?

— I know your son will not deny what he did, he loves me

— That's what we'll see. Marta, call Pedro immediately!

— Well, missus, excuse me!

The mistress and I sat there on that sofa in the spacious living room of the mansion where I worked for two years and lost my purity to a man who I believed loved me, was apprehensive, but sure that he would not deny taking on his responsibility. I had in my womb a child born with great affection, the fruit of our love.

— Mistress, here is your son!

— Sit down, Pedro!

— What is it about, Mom, what is this maid doing here?

— You should know, my son, is it not the father of the child she carries in her womb?

— What? But what a most unpleasant game is this, my mother, since when I didn't even touch that girl?

Pedro's reaction made the floor covered with a rich porcelain tile disappear under my feet, it was as if the whole world fell on my head, I lost all the security and tranquility of before, I saw my eyes wet with tears. end. The mistress, together with the housekeeper, looked at me puzzled by the boy's statements

— But what are you doing, baby, how do you say you never touched me? And how many times during these two years have you been lying with me in my room every night, making me swear of eternal love? Was it all a lie?

— Have you gone crazy, girl?

Did I ever go to your room or did I make any form of statements to you?

— Calm down my son!

I only called you here because this young woman said that since she arrived in this house that you have harassed her, having an intimate relationship that resulted in an unwanted pregnancy. As it is a serious myth, we needed to clarify this whole story immediately, since it contains the life of an innocent

— Mother, you and everyone here in this house know me, you know how irresponsible, fickle and judgmental I am about many things, but I would never commit such madness. How dare he harass a ten-year-old child and make him pregnant at twelve with so many women out there?

— I didn't believe a word of that girl, I always trusted her innocence, my son

— How can you act like that with me after everything we've lived together? You swore that you loved me, that you would never abandon me! Coward, he just wanted to abuse me and now he despises me with his son in his belly, damn miserable!

— Shut up, tomboy, and try to get out of that house immediately!

— Marta, get that girl out of the mansion, pay what you owe and have it returned to your parents. Inform them about the pregnancy and that the author is Pedro, son of the gardener, that they get along with the real responsible for the pregnancy of this inconsequential tomboy. Oh, and send the two employees away too to avoid future problems!

— As you wish, madam!

— Miserable, if you think things are going to be this way you are very wrong, you will pay dearly for what you did to me!

— How dare you still threaten my son, you worthless, out of this house!

— Yes, I will, you bastards, but you can wait for my revenge in all of your lives!

— Out of here!

While pouring out all the hate that burned inside her chest in front of those who acted unfairly with me, Marta pulled me by the arms in order to throw me out of the mansion.

After gathering my few belongings in a suitcase, I was driven by the housekeeper to my parents' house and handed over to my mother, as my father was not there at the time.

After shamelessly telling Mom the false story and throwing the poor boy a guilt he shouldn't have, he set off for the mansion, leaving behind a destroyed family.

— But my daughter, why did you allow this to happen to you? So much so that we advise you to take care of yourself, avoid this type of situation!

— Mother, it is as I just told you still in the presence of that unfortunate, the poor boy to whom she attributed this fault is innocent, the real father of that child is Pedro Dantas, son of the mistress!

— And do you keep insisting on this story, irresponsible girl, even after Dona Marta affirms that you got pregnant by the son of one of the employees there at the mansion?

— Yes, my mother! And I will die stating this version of the facts because that is the truth! They are millionaires, they are taking the child out of guilt because I am poor, they do not agree that he will marry a woman without a high position!

— Even if you're telling the truth how are we going to prove it? We do not have the resources to fight powerful people like the Dantas, my daughter, we will have to accept the damage and hope that this child will be born in peace

— No, Mom, I will never have peace until I demand this affront!

We were still talking when Dad came into the room, listening to part of what we were saying:

— My little girl, good to see you again! — Embraces me very tenderly — but what affront did you refer to when talking to your mother? Did someone humiliate my princess at the Dantas' mansion?

— Sit there, my husband, we have something very serious to solve

— What is it about, woman? Are you worrying me, did something serious happen to our daughter?

— Yes, father, it happened!

— Someone did you some evil, little daughter, tell me who is worthless and I swear I will receive the deserved punishment!

— Calm down, man, keep your feet on the ground because what we have to say is very serious!

Dad was a tall man, fair skin, full beard, yellow eyes.

Unusual, bored!His patience with anyone who did any harm to him or his family was zero. Because of that, he was very concerned about what his attitude would be after he became aware of what had happened, it certainly wouldn't be any good.

— Come on, you two, stop messing with me, what happened?

— Our daughter was abused ...

— Abused in what way?

— Sexually, man, she is two weeks pregnant and apparently there is confusion about who the child's father really is!

— How is it? Did you happen to lie down with several men as if you were some whore who doesn't even know who this poor child is who grows up in her womb?

My father got up from his chair, intending to give me a big beating, for the first time I saw that look of hatred on his face, his bulging eyes burned like flames of fire, I thought I wouldn't escape the beating. However, my mother stood between us and prevented the beating, I never imagined that such a loving father would dare to beat me.

— You prick! How dare you embarrass us that way?

— Calm down, man, she's our daughter!

— It doesn't seem like it, not after what you did!

— Let her explain herself first, listen to what she has to say then you will understand how it all happened!

Still breathing longing to break my face with punches.

And kicks he finally sat down again to listen to me, I remained silent with my head down in fear and respect until my mother ordered me to present my defense.

— Come on, Luana, tell your father your version of the facts!

I finally had the courage to reveal everything that happened to me in that damn mansion, detail by detail, without missing a single comma. Right away, my father believed my story, the opposite of Mom who listened to Marta, and burst into anger with a desire for revenge. It was exactly what we feared, because we knew how much he was an advocate for his family.

— Damn Dantas, they think they are too powerful to pay for their mistakes, because this time I will show them that my own justice will punish them!

— Calm down, darling, try not to rush!

— How can I remain calm after all that those people did to our daughter? Do you really think I'm going to sit idly while that kid has fun at the expense of other people's misfortunes?

— Dad, see what you're going to do, I also want revenge against that unfortunate, but we need to act with caution so that we don't bring any more problems to our home

— Paulo, if you attack that bastard in any way, his parents will even be able to have his life taken, think about it

— Jesus Christ, Dad, the mother is absolutely right, we don't want to lose you in the hands of those people! — Dad was warm-blooded, he was temperamental and without the least patience.

He didn't usually take offense without showing any reaction. He slept through the night and left the next morning before sunrise without saying where he was going, my mother and I believed he had gone to work, but we were wrong.

For years he kept a gun that had belonged to my grandfather, it was a cartridge of those very old, but well maintained, it worked very well. After loading it properly, he armed himself and went to stay at the point where Pedro always drove driving his luxury car in order to settle the score with the bastard, while he acted according to the burning anger in his heart we were apprehensive.

The bad character went to college and usually passed by the same avenue at that time which would facilitate the ambush, there were usually no security guards giving him protection, but due to the current situation two of them started to escort him, however, my father knew nothing about this change.

In the distance he saw when the vehicle was approaching and decided to act as soon as possible, he was hidden next to a curve that would force the driver to slow down and, when that happened, he took a direct hit in the direction of the car window, hitting the target. head of the driver who died instantly.

According to witnesses, Dad dropped his gun and ran towards a thicket near the place where he would have just committed the murder, however, the two men who came in another vehicle just behind followed him. The chase was closed, counting the two security guards, popular and the police the tragic end of this search for the killer was on the banks of a stream.

At least two kilometers from where the Dantas' son lost his life, as soon as he heard about it, his parents hired several other individuals who, armed to the teeth, entered the closed forest in order to kill my father at any cost.

While the deputy and his group of agents intended to capture him alive, the order of the Dantas was to be executed without mercy, the thirst for revenge was now rooted in them and no longer in us. We were warned about what happened and left in a hurry worried about what would happen to Dad. Deep down we could even imagine: Jail or death.

When we arrived at the indicated place we found a huge crowd of onlookers waiting for the outcome of that barbaric crime against one of the children of the most important family in the city, our presence was not even noticed by those who were there, since no one knew the criminal's real motivations when carrying out that one. shooting.

The day ended and with the arrival of the night without anyone returning from the forest with some news, the crowd gradually dispersed, only the two of us, some policemen and reporters who were covering the case, taking the information directly to the viewers in their homes across the state.

We returned home and watched the situation unfold on TV. Mom and I couldn't stop crying when we learned that if I was caught by the police, Dad would spend the rest of his life in jail. On the other hand, we were almost sure that if he were first captured by the men hired by the Dantas, his execution would be certain.The anguish felt by my poor mother changed her view of the facts and as a way to vent her pain she started to blame the blame for the misfortune that had befallen our family, which I thought was just.

After all, it was because of my inconsistency that I got my father into that hellish mess.

— It was all your fault! Paulo did not agree with the idea of you going to work in that damn mansion, but he ended up accepting only to not disappoint you, I was hoping for your happiness, I always wanted the best for you, now look at what happened for acting like a bitch, lying down with that wretch, we lost him!

— You are absolutely right, Mom, I am solely responsible for everything, it was my precipitations that put him in these conditions

— Good thing you recognize your mistake, because I will never forgive you for destroying our lives!

— Mom, don't be so cruel to me, I admit I was wrong, but don't condemn me that way

— What are you going to tell me? To claim that you committed this madness because you were only twelve years old? And where did all the good advice that Paulo and I gave you from when you were a child? Where were all of our guidelines for keeping that kind of man from? And what the hell was the fire between your legs that led you to this?

— I can not explain...

— Never before in my life have I heard that a ten-year-old girl felt sexual desire or that she could have sex for pleasure. This can only be the stuff of Satan in your life!

— Perhaps you are right ... But what your son did to me is also a big hooligan, lady!

32

— Look here, girl, listen to what I'm going to tell you with all your attention: After all this comes to an end, whether your father is arrested or dead, I want you to pack your bags and disappear from this house forever, understand?

— But, mother, where am I going to go in these conditions, pregnant without money, where am I going to stay?

— If you turn around, give your worthless way, my contempt will be the punishment you will receive for the great harm you caused us!

Hearing my mother's harsh words was terrible, it hurt my heart deeply, but I knew that deep down she was right to hate me so much. I was his biggest shame, his biggest disappointment, responsible for Dad's arrest or death, I really deserved his contempt. Throughout the night I did not take my eyes off the TV, sleep was gone and insomnia prevented me from sleeping.

I saw the hours passing slowly, it seemed like an eternity, she got a nap and rested a little from the rush of the previous day, then the morning newspaper duty announced that finally the search for the criminal had ended

As he would have been slaughtered in a confrontation with the police inside the forest. I woke up mom and we immediately headed to the place where it all happened, it was packed with people, we almost couldn't get close to the body, it was only possible after we proved to be her family.

Dad was all dirty, a huge amount of shots hit him from head to toe, in his right hand was a shotgun Everything was previously armed to hide what actually happened there.

As the police had already found the weapon used in the crime thrown by my father by the side of the road, was in the power of the deputy. How, then, did a rifle suddenly appear in his hand with which he confronted the police to the point of falling dead?

Certainly, the police chief and his companions received bribes to set up that shameful crime scene with the intention of deceiving the curious, the press and the criminal's relatives, no expertise was done because nothing could be revealed, once again the powerful won and the less favored were at a loss.

I was sorry to see my mother being thrown on her husband all riddled with bullets, I also hugged him and cried a lot about his death, many of the popular people who were touched by our pain gave us support, IML took the body to the morgue and then we veiled him in the chapel of the village where we lived. The funeral took place twenty-four hours later in a small public cemetery.

Only family members and few neighbors who knew him and knew of his moral integrity attended the funeral, Mom was inconsolable, my uncles and aunts wanted to eat me alive with their looks of revolt, because of that I stayed away from them during the entire wake and at procession to the place where he was buried.

As my mother had said, as soon as we returned home the whole family gathered in the small room, each of my uncles decided to agree to my immediate departure from my room, Mom would be taken with them and the property would be sold. The gesture of solidarity with my mother at that difficult time was very appropriate.

They were looking to profit at the expense of their pain, because even though we didn't have a decent house, the land was huge. Full of fruit trees, selling it would be easy and the value exorbitant. Mom always wanted to get rid of him to buy a better property in the city.

But Dad refused to let go of the inheritance left by my grandfather, now the tradition was being broken.She would be sold to strangers and not passed from father to son as she always did in the past, I was immensely saddened by all that, however, there was nothing I could do to prevent those poisonous snakes from taking over what would be my day by right.

After being judged and expelled from my own home, where I was born and lived part of my adolescence, I took courage, packed my bags and left aimlessly towards the unknown, waiting for what fate would have in store for the future. As I couldn't count on the support of family members, the way was to go to the passenger terminal, where I stayed for hours on end, it was after midnight, when a couple of tourists approached me.

And asked if I was staying there waiting for a relative or if the reason was because I had no right place to stay. I identified them as being gringos by their horrible accent and very peculiar appearance, I replied that I was lost, abandoned, that woman was moved when she heard my story and decided to help me, taking me with them to a five-star hotel located nearby.

There I was able to bathe, change clothes, have a delicious meal and rest. The next morning we went to one of the most exquisite stores in the city to shop. I moved in with them, as I was disowned by my family. Mrs Elisabeth was a very communicative, authoritarian woman, giving orders every minute to poor John, her husband who looked more like a dead slug.

However, despite the many differences they loved each other, they were happy. A month after my father's death, my mother told me to leave and to be trimmed by the English couple, it was time to make a very important decision in life, I had to choose between staying in my country or leaving him forever, because fate seemed to want to allow me to live new experiences.

— Luana, our time has come to leave for England, to return home, we have a lot of things to solve there, our tour is over

— I know that, Dona Elisabeth

— We propose you to come with us and give you time to think, well, we need to know what your decision was. Are you going with us to the UK or do you want to be close to your family?

— I have no family anymore, madam, they kicked me out of their midst, nor does my mother accept me as a daughter anymore

— Don't you think you should go and say goodbye to them anyway?

— No, I prefer to avoid disturbing them with my presence

— Very well, then we will take all the necessary measures to obtain your passport from the competent authorities and we will then leave

— It's ok

— And never say again that you have no family, because God has taken charge of putting you in our lives, that we also have no children, now we will be your parents and you our daughter

Elisabeth's words immensely comforted my heart.

Still bruised by the pain of losing my father, by the contempt of my mother and other family members, giving me the hope I needed to believe that I could still be happy.

— You can't imagine how happy I am to have met you

— We are lucky enough to meet you that night, dear

We traveled to the United Kingdom on a Saturday morning on a private flight, for the first time I was leaving my city to see the outside, during the trip I shook Elisabeth's hand strongly, shaking with fear for flying. Arriving at our destination, I marveled greatly at the beautiful view of London, one of the most beautiful capitals in the world.

My new friend and mother kept making fun of me, happily showing me every corner of the city, wishing to see me fully happy. John remained silent, sometimes let out a yellowish laugh, seemed too shy or closed to talk to me. Arriving at the address where we were going to form a new family, I admired so much luxury.

It was a huge mansion similar to that of Dantas, but belonging to super cool and admirable people who welcomed me, giving me a home to grow up and raise my son there. After being kindly received by the employees and housed in one of the many rooms in the house, after a deep rest I was invited to attend dinner.

— So, my dear, what did you think of your new home?

— Simply splendid, lady

— Please, from now on just call me Elisabeth

— It's ok

— And you can just call me John, without much formality

— Look, he finally said something! — I added — everyone there laughed at my observation, even John opened a broader laugh, showed that he liked my presence. In the days that followed, everything happened in complete peace and I visited several wonderful places.

Third Chapter: Visions of The Past

The British couple registered me as a legitimate daughter with great ease, due to the high knowledge and influence they had with the authorities, they intended to make me their only heir, owner of their many properties spread across the country. They also intended to recognize my son as a grandson who would be born in a few months.

However, fate once again resolved to prevent my happiness and I was encouraged to make a prank that was too expensive for all of us, as I invented riding a horse with no experience. Despite having the help of a professional I was unable to balance myself enough to avoid the tragic accident that resulted in an unexpected abortion.

The fall caused a heavy hemorrhage and as a result I lost the fetus growing in my womb, causing great pain and sadness for all of us who were waiting for it with anxiety. Elisabeth and John together with me wept over the loss of the baby, but on the other hand they made me understand that God was writing a new story for me there.

— My daughter, he knows what he does, surely this loss of yours can certainly mean the beginning of new conquests in your life

— Yes, I know I need to settle for all this

— Stay calm, baby, now it's up to you to move your head and move on, we have beautiful plans for you - John said

— Yes, Luana, we will put you to study in one of the most prestigious military schools in this country and there you will continue your path towards a promising future

— But I don't even know if I have a vocation for that kind of career!

— Well, if you find that you do not fit in the military area, you just finish your studies and you will be completely free to choose another professional area that you like

— All right, Elisabeth, I will do everything as you ask me

I started classes at the British Armed Forces school that same month and years later I was completing my high school education to the delight of my new parents. A big party took place in the mansion where we lived and many important guests were present, among them several politicians, businessmen, officers of the General Staff.

After spending several years among the military, I fell in love with the career and embraced it with all my heart, choosing the army as an area to act. After a selection test I joined as a sergeant, being immediately transferred to the training camp where the new officers were trained were prepared.

There I learned to use various firearms, I improved my aim considerably, I learned various techniques of fighting and self-defense, I participated in exhaustive combat training and because I did extremely successfully in all the tests I was submitted for, I went up in rank.

I was sent to a more advanced post as a lieutenant in the British Army and from then on my life would be profoundly transformed, because what awaited me up front would completely change the course of my existence. Due to so many responsibilities, I was seldom able to go to the mansion to visit Elisabeth and John, but that day news brought me to them.

— Lieutenant, correspondence for you

— Thank you, Sergeant

That sealed letter had a special recommendation written on its back, warning that it should be delivered exclusively in my hands and only read by me. When I received it I felt a chill inside me, it was as if something bad was kept inside it, so I opened it cautiously, since it was not usual to receive letters. After reading the few lines written on that letterhead, I could finally be sure that something very sad was waiting for me on the other side of that door, as soon as I left and returned to my house my heart would certainly be seriously hurt, something that had already become routine in my long-suffering existence.

I was not mistaken, John's call for me to come immediately to the mansion could only mean one thing: Something very serious would have happened to Elisabeth. Yes, in fact it was exactly that, she would be in very bad health. At least I still had the opportunity to see her before she left, a malignant tumor canceled her journey in this world. During my last visit Elisabeth asked me her last request, I wanted to forget a phrase that I never spoke to her, but at that moment I couldn't deny such a desire, since she welcomed me.Seeing her lying on that bed, practically lifeless, as if she was just waiting for my arrival moved me immensely.

When she approached me she opened a wide smile, asked for a hug and whispered in my ear with her voice almost silent:

— How good to see you, my daughter, nothing could make me happier in this painful moment in my life, thanks for finding time for one last goodbye. But, there's something I want to hear from your mouth before I leave

— Tell me, please, and I will certainly tell you

— I want to hear you call me mom only once, could you give me this last gift?

— Ah, mom, forgive me for all these years not recognizing the importance of this word for you, but know that even if you didn't pronounce it, it was always present in my thoughts, after all I owe everything to you and John, to whom today onwards I will call him father

— Good, daughter, because we also love her as if she were a legitimate daughter, with our blood running through her veins

— Yes, Elisabeth tells the truth, we never saw her as a child we adopted, but our only daughter

— I know, Dad, and I thank you so much for that

— You are very proud of us, daughter, you have become this brave, hardworking woman, winner after so many obstacles overcome

— I am honored to have you two in my life

In that atmosphere of love and family unity we hug and cry. A few days after my second mother passed away and we were at her funeral…

I urgently needed to return to the military base where I worked as a first lieutenant in special operations, my superiors reported that a war had started between England and the Argentines in search of dominance. over the Malvinas Islands. The political and commercial disagreement was due to the fact that the governments of the two countries disagreed over the territorial limit that divided the two nations, where the island in question served as a limit. The British claimed to be British-owned, while the Argentines insisted that they owned the right to possession.

In fact, the dispute had nothing to do only with the territorial limit, but because of the immense amount of oil there, which certainly meant a real gold mine that would further enrich the country that exploited it. In that way, a fierce battle between the two nations has been fought since then and my mission was to urgently go to confrontation.

A battalion of men extremely well trained in the art of war was entrusted to me and in a few hours after receiving the necessary instructions we were already flying towards the battle point. Once we got there, we started the confrontation, since several other groups of soldiers were already confronting the enemy with great success. We had only had small casualties, nothing to worry us about a defeat, although we were very sorry for the loss of our combat brothers.

— Quick, let's not give the enemy any respite, let's show what we are capable of! Sergeant, take your men to the right side of the island, the rest come with me!

— Yes, Lieutenant! You heard the order given, men, let's put these worms to run back to the land they came from!

We acted fiercely against opponents who retreated with each blast of bullets from our weapons, but we cannot deny their fiery courage in facing us. The British army was much more equipped with state-of-the-art weapons, much more modern weapons and surprising technology.

In fact, we took the opportunity to test several of them recently built by our Technological Engineering Center and despite the Argentine resistance we easily detonated all of its military bases previously established on the island. As I mentioned before, we had casualties, we lost many friends in that bloody battle, but we won.

The 75-day war ended only on June 14, with the Argentines surrendering. In all, 258 Britons and 649 Argentines died in the conflict. Diplomatic relations between the United Kingdom and Argentina were only resumed in 1990, but there are still strikes, but that was impossible to avoid when our objective was to conquer those lands.

After the victory over our opponents, we returned to the Northern Military Base, where each platoon acted, after receiving the formal praise of my superiors for the success obtained in the mission, I resumed my internal functions as chief engineer in the line of creation and assembly of war armaments.

I was also allowed to go to the mansion to see my father, who was already well in days, so it was possible to kill the nostalgia and see how proud he was of the woman I became, especially after the last achievement achieved.

— Daughter, you only make me proud!

— Thank you Dad!

— I followed on TV news the fight between you and the Argentines, how they massacred you!

— Actually, Dad, they proved to be true warriors, because they fought with us as equals. They only lost the war because we were better armed than they were, otherwise I don't know how it would all end

— It may be, daughter, but I still believe that we Britons are several steps above their military experience. England has a history of wars in its curriculum, we have already participated in important battles in the history of mankind, such as the Second World War. And what about the Argentines, what great deeds do they have to rejoice in defense of their country and the world?

— Well, maybe now they can be proud of something

— A tiny pride in what we have

Dad was an Englishman in love with his homeland, a millionaire who always invested his wealth in the nation where he was born, grew up and would certainly die, despite how a good tourist got to know the whole world in his dozens of trips around the world together with his beloved wife . I admired him too, I would like to know how to demonstrate this more clearly.

Returning to the Military Base, I was again asked to appear before my superiors with the greatest urgency, as I was informed that they intended to send me on a new mission.

— Sit down, Lieutenant, we need you to carry out a new mission in defense of our country.

This time in Ukraine, since you are the most suitable person to carry it out, taking into account the enormous success achieved in the recent field battle, making it the most excellent of all. We want to know your willingness to accept it

— Of course, Colonel, and what is it about?

— This time it is not a war like the one you participated in a short time ago, but a rescue mission

— Rescue, sir? Can I know who we're talking about?

— He is a very important man for our nation, as he is well connected politically with the great world powers, including the USA, which will also be sending some of its best agents to free him

— You will be joining the CIA to assist the Special Forces in rescuing the prisoner — Major Willis warned me

— Yes, sir, I understand. And who will be in charge of this mission, us or the CIA?

— They are, of course, but it is you who they want to be assigned to lead the agents who will execute it — Colonel David clarified to me

— But with so many well-trained agents with more experience than I in American Intelligence, why did you choose me to lead such an important mission, sir?

— After its performance in the recent war it was targeted by the Americans

— Thank you, sir, I'm flattered

— They believe that the success achieved in that battle was due to the war strategy used by you in the leadership of the platoons in combat and this is something we cannot deny, because your performance was really splendid, in addition to the high level of training you received , gaining the most prominence at the British Army Academy, something never given to a woman before — completed Willis

— Feel yourself, Lieutenant, because inexplicably you have demonstrated an admirable gift for combat, your goals achieved in training were able to overcome even many of our best men, we are sure that you are ready to perform this important mission.

— In fact, Lieutenant, although we are aware of your little performance in special missions like this, we are sure that you will do very well, this will be just another one of your great achievements that will appear in your military curriculum.

— Thanks again, gentlemen, I will be available to start my new job

— Very well, you should report to the Major Command of the Armed Forces in London tomorrow, where you will receive the award deserved for your recent combat activity in the Falkland Islands and then you will depart on a private flight to New York.

— A decoration, sir?

— Yes, it will move from the current rank of lieutenant to Lieutenant Colonel

— Thank you, sir

— Don't thank him, he did it well.

And if he returns from his first mission as an agent with the same success obtained in the war fought in the Malvinas, he will rise to the rank of Major. Now you are excused, get ready for the trip that must be done tomorrow morning, very early. An aircraft will be waiting for you at the Aeronautics airport

— Yes sir

It is neither necessary nor detailed here the emotion that I felt when I learned that I would be leveling up within the Armed Forces, my father would be red with pride and happiness for these achievements. But he deserved all that joy for having extended his hands to me in the most tragic moment of my life.

The only sadness I had on my chest was for Elisabeth. It took me too long to call her a mother, years passed and I was never able to pronounce this word for her to hear, perhaps because I was deeply disappointed with the attitude taken by the one who brought me into the world, for having driven me out of the house without giving the chance of regret for what I let happen in our family.

The word "mother" has become bitter on my palate for decades, so how could I use it when referring to the one she welcomed as a daughter and heir to all her possessions? Speaking of which, assets that I didn't know how to manage after John's death, I would have to entrust to strangers, because I understood nothing about management. But, okay, I would stop worrying about these details later, at the moment I had to focus on the mission, rescuing that influential man for the two governments, American and British, was at that moment the most important thing to do.

There was no time to go to the mansion to explain everything to Dad, nor could I do that, because that mission was secret, any vacillation could leak and fall into the enemy's knowledge. Early in the morning, I showed up at the Air Force Base and was taken in a private jet to present myself at the American Intelligence, who were waiting for me beforehand.

— Good morning, I'm Lieutenant Colonel Luana, I came on behalf of my country to collaborate with the important rescue mission that American Intelligence will carry out

— Yes, we are aware of your coming, we will let you know all the information we have about the exact location of the victim to be rescued and the best way to get through security, entering the place without being seen

In a few minutes I was on top of all the necessary information, I was properly presented to the agents I was going to work with, we received guidance on how to act, what to avoid, the duration of the action and the extraction point where we would be rescued after success of the mission.

— Well, this is what we had to provide you with guidelines, we wish you success!

— Thank you, sir, we'll be back soon

— Sure, come back alive

— Certainly, sir, our main priority is to rescue the prisoner alive and get here on time

Ten highly trained agents were entrusted to me for that mission in Ukraine.

An important Diplomat had been kidnapped and was held captive in a secret location located in the basement of an old building on the outskirts of KIEV, the country's capital with about 2 611 327 inhabitants. We had in hand the defined map of its location and a drawn plan.

However, there was a somewhat harsh atmosphere among the team destined to accompany me on that mission, since among the ten agents, three were women much more experienced than I in that type of task and refused to receive my orders. The one who least accepted me as a leader was Sophia, an impressive-looking woman with a high level of military training.

He had already commanded several troops in important battles while he was in the American Navy, reached the rank of Major and after they transferred him to the CIA, he stood out immensely among the other colleagues, his dissatisfaction was even understandable, because she was the one who should command that mission, but they chose me. They commented during the trip in a low tone, almost babbling.

— I can't accept all this cardboard from our superiors, is there no one at the Agency prepared enough to carry out this rescue that they were forced to bring a beginner to lead us? — Complained Sophia

— I don't understand it either, but if these are the orders, we should follow them without arguing — added one of them

— Maybe you passively accept this situation, but I don't

— And what are you going to do, disobey superior orders?

— After we arrive in Ukraine I will put into practice all my experience as an agent, I will not be under the command of a newbie

— You are the one who knows, but this attitude will cost you dearly, maybe even a shutdown of operations or the definitive exclusion from the Organization

The conversation between the women continued until we arrived in Ukraine, where we were awaited by a team of other agents who had already carried out the necessary investigations of the place where the man was kept in captivity. After a thorough explanation of the current situation made by colleagues, we left to carry out the mission given to us.

Aware of what we would find ahead, we divided into two groups, putting the rescue operation into practice, I followed with five agents and the rest were under the command of Sophia who was surprised by my way of acting. Having heard her say that she was much more capable than I was to carry out the mission, I gave her the opportunity to show her worth.

— We will divide into two groups to surround the place on both sides and surprise the kidnappers, five of you will follow Sophia and the rest will come with me!

— All right, guys, you heard the lieutenant, come on!

We walked through a dark and narrow space in the direction informed by the Intelligence as the exact point of captivity, we could not put the Diplomat's life at risk, so I recommended to the agents that they avoid direct confrontation with the bandits while the victim was not safe. The plan was for the team led by Sophia to rescue the prisoner, avoiding the maximum exchange of fire, for this to happen, it would be necessary for us to get the criminals' attention.

So that they would turn to us while the other team released the hostage. Minutes later we were at the indicated point, from there we could see the prisoner sitting on a chair, tied feet and hands, blindfolded and four well-armed men around.

I also saw our colleagues who stood on the right side of the captivity, waiting for my signal to act, we were all ready to take action. However, our plans were thwarted by the unexpected arrival of several other bandits who decided to remove the victim from there, taking him to another location, they seemed to be aware of our presence.

In Ukrainian they talked to each other, but as we all spoke several languages we understood perfectly what they were saying to each other, somehow they were informed of our arrival there and were organizing themselves to not allow us to return alive. My colleagues were in favor of the two groups coming together again and facing the enemy.

— The victim is no longer here, there is no more risk of him being injured, so let's detonate these scoundrels and see if there is still time to find him in another part of that filthy hole! — Advised one of them

— I agree, let's get together with the other agents and put them on top of those scoundrels! — Opinioned the other

— All right, we need to act fast before they get you out of here and take you to an unknown location

In a short time we were back in number of ten agents and we strictly followed the plan to eliminate the enemy.It didn't take long for us to be received under a real rain of bullets.

In the underground corridors where we passed, because of our extreme defense capacity we were not shot down one by one. Sophia really had the training she claimed to have, she knew how to properly use a gun with accurate shots.

In addition to counting on his vast experience and that of everyone else, I also played my part in the fight against those bandits, we took down many of them in a short time and without casualties. When we arrived in a wide space, after a long exchange of shots, almost without ammunition, we had to use another strategy to defeat them completely.

Thus, sometimes we saved ammunition and went on a close combat, it was the moment when we put to the test all our experience acquired during training in the academy, because in war this is not always possible. At one point my colleagues were surprised by my fighting techniques.

In others, they were excellent fighters. In the end the Ukrainians were defeated, but the target of our mission had been taken to an unknown location and that meant that we would have to stay there for longer than anticipated. We reported the inconvenience to our superiors at the CIA and received authorization to continue.

— But what a beautiful performance, Lieutenant, admirable your self-defense techniques — one of them praised me

— Thanks! You were also great

— We all did well, but we didn't finish the mission!

— Relax, Sophia, we'll get them soon and free that diplomat!

— Don't let your guard down, we are in the enemy's sights!

Abdenal Carvalho

Sophia was still bitter, annoyed that she was refused by the Agency to lead the team, but that did not disturb me, because it is common for other people's jealousy, when you reach a level in life where your brilliance overshadows those who, despite your efforts, seem not to get out of place.

That night we remained hidden in the ruins of the old buildings that always surrounded us with our eyes wide open to avoid any surprise, while the Agency used all technological means to locate the whereabouts of those who fled taking the Diplomat. We did three shifts every two hours, in the meantime I fell asleep.

When I closed my eyes, I started to have strange visions like I never had before, it didn't seem like a common dream, it was as if it really happened to me. At one point I was in a bloody battle with several enemies with extraordinary powers, I was a warrior whose sword dissipated them all.

The scenario recalled the epic medieval times, where the weapon used were spears and swords, I dressed in a breastplate that protected the whole body against frequent attacks, in that battle where many bodies fell lifeless at my feet with their heads cut into a river of blood was formed, there were countless those who went on to the hereafter.

While they were maimed by the sharp blade of my sword, I looked around and saw other warriors who also faced the band of giants, seemed to respond to my command, I led them. As a powerful warrior fought against my opponents with immense courage and was successful in all the attacks, always accompanied by my allies, who equally feared nothing, we advanced towards the army of thugs without giving them a second of truce, he didn't quite understand what a fierce battle it was or why, however.

He understood that it was something to be done, he would have a good reason, a necessary cause, so he went on beheading one by one of those who dared to cross my path. At another point the scene changed and I found myself in the abyss, in the center of the earth, in a place where volcanic lava flowed all over the place, people chained, suffering, enslaved.

There were huge ditches that served as prisons for men and women whose condemnation was not revealed to me, they lived there for a long time in chains, a huge amount of filthy waste dripped into those holes day and night, filling them up to their height. necks, making it almost impossible to breathe.

Around all those underground prisons were several beings with their pointed spears in their hands, others with bows and arrows, huge axes and sickles, sharpened as never before, guarding each pit where the prisoners were. As if taking a walk around the place, I came across spacious corridors where I could see barred cells.

Inside were other individuals standing, chained by wrists and ankles, their bodies were stretched to such an extent that it was possible to see their ribs exposed on the skin. At another point in the place I came across some who were tied to the trunk, being whipped by the executioners who pulled pieces of their back with their steel whips.

Their screams echoed through the rocky walls of that place that looked like hell itself, I strolled there without being noticed by someone, scary beings passed by me every second, from side to side, always armed, with their monstrous faces and flaming looks like flames of fire.I followed more and more into that accursed place as if I was being driven to reach its end.

By an unknown force, each part found seeing tragedies, pains, sufferings and the terror that spread everywhere. Suddenly I heard the sound of a voice similar to a very loud roar that greeted me, ordering me to come closer.

— Hail, Queen, how nice to see you back at your house!

I was startled by that booming voice and confused by his declaration that he would be back at my house, after all, what the hell was this pointless conversation? Me, belonging to that hellish place? Since when? I complied with his mandate and went in the direction of something similar to a giant throne, on which sat a monstrous being.

As I got a little closer, I could see his appearance better, he had a strange physiognomy, his face was of a pig, the feet and hands of a frog, his skin was scaly as if it were a fish and his eyes were burning red hot. A tongue similar to that of tadpoles came out of his mouth, he was at least two and a half meters tall, maybe even a little more than that.

He wore a crown of yellow metal on his head, looked like gold, held something like a staff with a skull in his right hand, dressed like a king and acted in such a way that his subjects obeyed him without any resistance, continued with his comment:

— I knew that one day I would return, we were waiting for you, welcome back, your kingdom has been waiting for you since your departure

— Sorry, but I don't remember ever being here, even if I met you, how do you call me Queen and say this is my home?

— It is quite natural that your doubt as to what is evident in your eyes, my dear, but it is all true, you have always belonged to this place…

56

And your presence here today proves it

— Actually, I don't even know why this happened, because I was meeting with my agents on an important mission, when I suddenly fell asleep and was taken to a battlefield in an unknown place, when I suddenly came here. Is this a dream?

— You find yourself in the mortal world in a second reincarnation after having rebelled against your own kingdom and held captive in the lower regions of the earth, among those condemned to eternal death. By her own choice she turned against me, her husband, choosing to follow that Archangel against whom all our legions fought without success.

When she was taken by him to the Higher Kingdom, she was forgiven of all her sins and sent to a new existence in the world of mortals, dedicated to a chaste, pure life, avoided how she could have sex, became holy before human beings due to his immense dedication to the poorest.

However, it seems that she made the mistake of practicing idolatry, a sin considered one of the greatest abominations by the Creator, so she was banished from Paradise to a new life on earth. Today you have a new name, you live a new history, but before you were my Queen, wife, together we were responsible for many catastrophes, destruction and corruption of mankind.

— If what you say is true, why can't I remember these details?

— Very simple, when the spirit is reincarnated it receives a new body, the mind is empty and nothing that lived in previous lives can be remembered.

However, in some cases where reincarnations are multiple, he may have certain lapses of memories that manifest during sleep, as in your case

— So I'm actually sleeping right now?

— Your physical body yes, however, you are truly here in spirit which is your true essence

— And who are you, anyway?

— There was a time when I was called Lucifer, one of the first inhabitants of Eden, the garden of the Creator

— I have heard of you, my parents were very religious and taught me about your story found in the Bible, it is the Anointed Cherub of God who rebelled and was banished from heaven together with thousands of angels who supported his rebellion against the Most High

— Yes, in fact, today I am known both in the world of mortals and in the spiritual world as Satan, the accuser, the devil, the prince of darkness, the worst enemy of God, the one who introduced sin into this world, the father of lies, responsible for the degradation of mankind. There are many attributions that they make to me due to the most varied forms of evil that spread among humanity. And you, my dear, have always been by my side for about two centuries, helping to dismantle the Creator's works. During her first two reincarnations in the outside world became the greatest of all prostitutes on earth, corrupting humanity.

His greatest performance in this regard was as Pomba-Gira, the Queen of prostitutes, from time to time he rose to the surface to incite men and women in the practice of sexual immorality, through prostitution, adultery.

Pornography, pedophilia, lust and homosexuality. All those who followed after your advice are here, doomed.

— And after I rebelled against this kingdom of darkness and was rescued by the Most High, did this evil cease to exist on earth?

— No, because the evil that we spread in humanity took root in the heart of man and even when we are not inciting them to sin they do so deliberately

— Apparently taking me out of here and taking me to paradise, granting a new opportunity for existence is of no use to change the moral character of humanity, is it still lost, walking towards hell?

— Certainly, yes. Since the beginning of Creation, the Creator has been trying to have for himself a holy people who could praise and magnify his holy name in the Universe, particularly on earth. First he made us, his separate angels for praise, I was his singing master. But the glory he gave me was so great that I was exalted, I wanted to expel him from the throne and take his Kingdom by force. However, I failed in front of his most powerful Archangel and I was cast down with my allies. All planets, stars, celestial stars, nature itself are the work of his hands and revere him, but man was easily corrupted by me in the garden. Never again being able to give him the deserved adoration, so even with the sacrifice made by his Son on the Cross he was totally successful at it

— It is true, evil continues to reign sovereignly over the earth

— We know that very soon we will be destroyed, he will finally destroy evil, we will all be thrown into the Fire that will burn forever, but until that day will come we will continue to lead man to sin.

Increasing in the greatest possible number of those who will descend with us into the lava fiery

— My goodness, that means that I will also burn in the eternal flames!

— For sure!

His last words thundered so loudly that I felt the ground under my feet shudder. After that, I was transported to a new scenario, where for a few seconds I found myself in front of a shining angel who cried out, saying to me: "Strive, strive, seek God and avoid eternal death!".

I saw before me a great white throne and seated on him was the righteous and holy. All men, large and small, appeared before him to account for their deeds through the bodies they received from him to live on earth. A large book was opened, an angel read its pages, citing those written on it. However, all who did not have their names written in the Lamb's Book of Life perished. They were expelled from his presence, thrown into the Lake of Fire created by God for Satan.

Together with all your fallen angels and those who chose to follow your sinful precepts. On the right, left and behind the throne several glorious living beings glorified God. They shouted loud and clear with their booming voices: "Holy, holy is the Lord of heaven and earth who will reign forever, for he has been given all dominion and nothing will resist his infinite power !!!" Still hearing these strong words, I moved away from there, gradually waking up and returning to reality, being bothered by one of the agents.

— Lieutenant, Lieutenant, wake up!

— What is it, man, what nonsense is this?

— Enemies approaching from all sides!

The night was still dense in darkness and the sun seemed to be slow to rise, we were surrounded within the ruins of that old building, we needed to defend ourselves from the attack that was coming our way. We divided into small groups and we tried to receive the invaders with the right bullets so that they would be immediately slaughtered. The advantage was that the whole team had good aim, in addition to extremely efficient training in hand-to-hand combat and that made a difference. When our enemies invaded the place, thinking they would take us by surprise, they were shot and killed. About thirty bandits were no match for a contingent of just ten.

— Madam, we caught one of them alive!

— Okay, well, let's force him to reveal where the prisoner was taken!

— Right!

The man was tortured by one of our own until he said the exact location of the current captivity, and then he was executed. We headed for the location after informing the base of our new position. In order for them to send reinforcements, if necessary, or to define a new rescue point after the mission is completed.

We arrived at the indicated point in at least an hour and separated again into small groups for greater success of the action. Sophia and two other agents followed on the left, me and others on the right. The others at the rear, the atmosphere was hostile, closely watched, but we would certainly take care of them all. We use pistols with mufflers to avoid attracting the attention of the guards, when possible we would only use our fighting skills.

At first it was very easy to dominate them without attracting attention, but when we tried to enter the captivity we were noticed. The direct confrontation based on many shots became inevitable, so we had to defend ourselves at height.

Using large caliber weapons as the situation demanded, fighting an intense battle with the few who still resisted, we finally saw the last of them fall to the ground and we breathe a sigh of relief to see that the hostage has not suffered any injuries.

Despite the rain of bullets that occurred at the site. After successfully rescuing the Diplomat, we took him to the combined extraction point with the Agency and returned safe and sound without any casualties. When we arrived in the capital of New York, we were immediately asked to present ourselves to our superiors to receive their congratulations on the success of the mission.

— Congratulations on the success achieved in your first mission through the Agency, Lieutenant, we are really satisfied with the results. We see that the recommendations about him were true

— Thank you, sir, but I would have done nothing without the help of all my colleagues who are here. The skill, experience and companionship of all of them, together with our joint efforts, has resulted in this success

— Very well, Lieutenant, I see that besides being very efficient, you have the humility of not wanting only the glory of this great success for yourself. Well, you're all excused, take a few days off

— Thank you sir!

We are entitled to relax in whatever way we prefer for three days from that day. As it was a Saturday, I was invited by the team to go and enjoy the night in one of the many nightclubs in the New York capital, one of the largest and most beautiful cities on the planet. I loved being in a place like that, higher than London.

During the fun, while we danced to one of the beautiful American songs Sophia approached me, took one of my hands and took me to a small space located outside the dance house. I thought her attitude towards me was strange, after all, since we met, I only saw her dislike for me, but I respected the moment.

Arriving where she wanted us to be, she looked at me with a less aggressive look, opened a wide smile and hugged me. Not knowing what to do, completely surprised, I responded without much emotion, making her realize my bewilderment. But that was normal, since I could barely predict that she would suddenly take such an action, as it seemed that the possibility of understanding between us was remote.

— I know that I am being inappropriate in my attitudes, after all, until a few hours ago I was rude to you for imagining that I was being wronged by the loss of command of the team. But after seeing his humility in defending our importance with the great success achieved in the mission, not only requiring all privileges for himself, I recognized my mistake and here I am to apologize

— There was no need for that

— Of course, because I was unfair to you.

It was not your fault if the Agency preferred to entrust the command of the mission to you than to pass it on to any of its best agents

— To be honest, I didn't understand why, I know how much everyone has been dedicated to the Agency and deserve an opportunity like this, including you who, as far as I know, have even led several previous missions and with good results

— Yes, it's true, but that's exactly why I now recognize how selfish I was

— I didn't see your attitude that way, just felt diminished

— Nothing, it was more than that, I was proud to think I was more capable than a newbie to lead the team, I underestimated you

— Okay, but in any case we must forget about this episode and move on, we will make things different between the two of us going forward, right?

— Of course, that's why I brought you here, I really want peace and friendship between us

— Friends, then?

— I'm certainly not one to hold grudges

We went back inside the club and there we drank, danced, smiled a lot at our bullshit all night and in the morning I went to Hotel Plaza, where I was staying until the Agency dismissed me and I could go back to the Army Base in London, where I worked in my duties. However, different from what I expected the next morning, still a bit hungover from the night of drunkenness the night before. I received a call from my superiors saying that I would have to stay in New York for a few more days.

Requiring my urgent presence at the headquarters of the A few minutes later, I was visited by an agent who took me there.

— Welcome back, Major!

— Sorry, sir, but I think there was a mistake about my patent. I'm a lieutenant in the American Armed Forces

— No more, due to the excellent work done to our country, we want to have the honor of telling you that your patent has been changed to Major and from now on you will no longer render your military services in London, but will become an exclusive agent of that Agency. Intelligence.

The declarations of one of the highest CIA ranks left me with my feet high, I never thought I would receive such an honor, since anyone would want to gain such an important position in his career as a member of the Armed Forces. When John and Elisabeth said they were going to adopt me I thought they lived in the USA, but I was wrong.

It has always been my dream to live in New York, since I reached the age of majority and now at twenty-five years of age I did it splendidly. John would certainly be proud of my latest achievements, but at the same time saddened by the distance that would separate us, however, it was his desire to see me grow in the career I chose. After the formalities, I returned to the hotel to continue my due rest, aware that in two days the break would end and I should receive from the Agency a new mission in the company of a group formed by the best agents of the corporation. I took the time off and with the Agency's permission I returned to London to tell John the news.

— My daughter, what a nice surprise to see you again!

— Likewise, Dad!

— But come on, my dear, tell me all about the latest news

— Yes, I'll tell you everything

We spent part of the night talking and I made him aware of all the changes that have taken place in my life in the past few weeks, including my unexpected summons to take up residence in New York and establish my role as an agent at the American Intelligence Agency.

— My God, daughter, how far you have come, your mother would be very proud of you, just as I am

— Sorry, Dad, I know say that with a broken heart

— Certainly it will not be easy for me to go months without seeing you, knowing that your current role will put you at greater risk every day and will bring me great anguish, yet I fully support your decision to take this further step in your career. I will not use selfishness, thinking only of my own happiness of having her around

— I knew I could count on your support my father

— I promised to always be by your side, daughter, whatever it was

— That's why I love you so much

— I love you too, baby, but since we are having this conversation…

Tell me: How will things be in relation to our assets now that you intend to dedicate yourself exclusively to the Agency?

— Daddy, you always knew that I never intended to run your companies.

Or any other asset you own, in my opinion you should continue to be responsible for reliable people who have been helping you in this area for so many years

— It turns out that I'm not that young anymore, daughter, I need a successor in business, I can't just donate my goods to charity, after all, that's why God or destiny put you in our lives, to inherit the fruit of so much work that your mother and I did in building this immense heritage. We need to come to a good sense to know what to do from now on, I need you to help me decide

— You will still live for a long time, you grumpy old man, you have an iron health! — Laughs

— Maybe so, I always kept myself from exaggeration, I didn't have any addiction and I value every second of my life, that's why I care for my health above all. However, even so, time goes by and I grow older every day

— Let's do this, Daddy, I will agree with everything you choose to do from now on, if you decide to keep all your assets so when you leave I see what I do with them all right, but if your choice is to sell them I will too I agree

— Very well, I'll think about what to do and then we'll talk

— That's how we talk, don't worry because we will still talk for a long time

We spent the last two days of my CIA leave together at the mansion and then returned to New York to attend the Agency. There I was informed that my old team and I would meet again on other missions.

Indeed, this has happened dozens of times and in all of them we have had great successes without any losses among our people. With so many comings and goings we ended up becoming so fond of ourselves that we love each other like real brothers.

We started to be seen by the Agency as the best trained operations group for the most important missions, where we never failed, we went from an experimental team to the most prestigious within Intelligence.

Fourth Chapter: Operation Bosnia

Sophia and I, who didn't get on very well before, now we end up becoming confidants, revealing some secrets to each other. In fact, she told me more about herself because she had more experiences in the love life and her stories served as examples for me not to make the same mistakes in the future.

I told him about my first disappointment in love, the decision never to delude myself again with false promises of eternal union or to believe in the words of a man, the brutal way my family treated me after my father's death, the expulsion of home for mom, the luck I had to be rescued by John and Elisabeth.

How they raised and educated me as if they were their blood daughter, the great opportunity to join the British Armed Forces, then my trip to the CIA where we met. The boys and other colleagues with whom we worked on the missions also became very close, we formed a very close and receptive group.

One night after returning from a mission in Iran I was lying in my bed, when I suddenly fell asleep and was taken once again in spirit to the lowest regions of the earth. There I returned to be face to face with the DEMO that made me a terrifying revelation, stating that soon I would be confronted by the darkness. He told me that he had sent one of his sons to reincarnate on earth — in fact only considered by him as more special demons.

Since the Devil cannot bear children — and that he became someone very important in the world of crime, making him if the biggest and worst drug dealer, weapons, human beings. Terrifying several nations, taking terror to the four corners of the earth, challenging any authority with its army of hundreds of men well trained to fight, armed to the teeth, fierce, determined, unable to be afraid of any enemy that confronted.

That vision of hell lasted only a few minutes and soon I woke up, I was still dressed in my clothes used on the trip of the previous day, as I was barely able to get to my apartment where I threw myself on the bed immensely tired. When I woke up, panting, due to the hellish vision I had, I remained for a few minutes sitting by the bed disturbed.

When I had such visions the first time and there I talked with the one who identified himself as Satan, I was doubtful, I thought it was just a dream although quite real, but now for the second time I was facing that evil being whose words made the most sense, since there was even an individual in the East whose characteristics matched his description.

Our superiors at the Agency had already informed us of his work in the world of crime and the way he spread terror wherever he went, several divisions of Special Forces from different nations tried to fight it without success, the world was scared by his criminal performance, it seemed almost impossible to stop it. I spent the rest of the night in the open due to the damn insomnia that usually plagued me after a nightmare. So I took the opportunity to feed it even more, drinking one cup of coffee after another until I saw the sunrise. I thought about talking to my colleagues about those visions that had been disturbing my mind.

Maybe that would ease my tension, however, giving up on that, since few people believe in the supernatural, they might even see me as crazy and if the Agency even imagined from afar that one of its agents was hallucinating, he would be immediately removed from his duties to undergo psychiatric treatment.

We were good friends until then, but who could guarantee that everyone would keep it a secret? The human heart is full of unpleasant surprises, when it is least expected it can surprise us in a dangerous and destructive way. So I chose to silence, to keep only those revelations from hell to myself.

"Good morning, gentlemen, I summoned the presence of all of you here to let you know about the most recent events around the world, about the need that we have to continue combating the threats that arise day after day against world peace. So, observe in these images acquired via satellite the destruction caused by our current enemy. According to our intelligence, he started his criminal action in Bosnia, particularly in Sarajevo, extending it to other cities until he became stronger to the point of dominating the whole country. With the support of influential people in all social and political areas, he managed to cross borders, reaching several other nations around the world. Our new mission is to find the weak point of your organization so that you can destroy it, putting an end to its criminal actions that have put the governments of the world on alert. However, this time we will act differently, we will select only two of our best field agents to carry out this task."

— Only two agents, sir?

— Yes, Major, it will be enough!

— We do not intend to come into direct confrontation with the enemy because we know he is highly dangerous. Many troops have already been decimated by their army before they even started the battle, their attacking fronts are being considered invincible or impenetrable. What we want is for these two agents to enter the wolf's lair and dismantle their defenses so that our best war platoons can defeat them in combat. This bastard, along with everyone who follows him, must have a weakness!

— Certainly sir!

— Our Intelligence Base joined with all the others existing on the four Continents to gather information about who their allies are so that they can be arrested as soon as possible, as we understand that for him to know the exact moment of our air, water or land attacks it's because someone tells you about our plans. While Intelligence works on this particular point, two of our best agents will infiltrate the lair, understand?

— Yes sir!!!

— Very well, dismissed, wait for instructions!

While we waited for the final decision of the Intelligence Department, they analyzed the best strategy to start the operation, however, there were differences of opinion:

— In my opinion, sending two agents at once to infiltrate PETROVIC's criminal organization is ineffective — said one of them

— And for what reason do you think so? — Asked the biggest leader of the Agency

— One can delay the other…

Besides that it would be a great waste to lose both at once, taking into account being the best among those we have

— I totally agree, the ideal is to send one first and then the other, in case the first one fails in his mission — another said

— Very well, and what others think here?

— We also agree with the suggestion! — added a third person, speaking on behalf of the others

After three days we were summoned to appear before our superior to receive the necessary instructions, which did not take longer than expected and soon we were back at CIA Headquarters.

— Welcome back gentlemen, have a seat! We have already reached a definitive conclusion as to how the next mission will be carried out and by whom. We will inform you which of you will receive such responsibility

— What do you mean, sir, wouldn't two agents be sent on this mission? — I asked

— At first yes, but in common agreement we understand that it is not effective

— In my opinion two would be ideal because they could act separately at two points at the same time

— Certainly, Major, but the risks of losing them at once if something goes wrong are huge, remember that we will be sending our best men to fulfill this mission and that would be a great loss for our Agency

— I understand, sir

— Okay, does anyone else have anything to add? — Everyone's silence answered his question — Ok, so we will announce the name of the one who will be sent to Sarajevo today!

The CIA general secretary approaches us all, distributes small black folders and asks us to wait for instructions, then one of our superiors orders us to open them.

— Open the folder in your possession, only one of which contains detailed information about the secret mission that one of you will carry out from now on, good luck!

I was almost sure that Sophia and I were going to be sent to Bosnia, but after learning that the Agency opted to send just one agent, I had no idea which one of us would be chosen. Sophia looks at me happily and I soon saw that she would have been chosen for that important mission, however, I was very worried. Despite the improved training of my youngest friend, I felt that she would not be completely able to solve that task alone, they were sending the agent they saw as the second best as bait.

Well, I couldn't say that to her because she would certainly be pissed off at me, would call me envious, that I would be upset that I hadn't been chosen and all. So I found it convenient to support her in that moment that seemed to be the height of her career as an agent. His trip took place that same night, we said goodbye warmly.

— Have a nice trip, my friend, I will be rooting for you

— Thank you, Luana, counting on your support at a time like this is very important

— Take care, please come back alive

— I promise to do everything possible so that soon we are all together to celebrate the success of this mission

After a strong hug she was gone, I spent the whole night dominated by worry and insomnia took over me, something told me that things would not end well for my friend. Now I could understand what John felt at every moment that he didn't see me around, it was a terrible feeling. The next morning I met Richard at a coffee shop located a few steps from the building where I lived and passed for some civilian.

— Don't worry, Sophia is one of the most experienced and well-trained agents we had here before you arrived. She has already carried out several other missions in which she has worked very successfully on her own, for sure this will be just one more that will enter her vast curriculum

— I hope you're right about that, Richard

— I am, you will see!

The conversation with my friend was long, productive and pleasant, he was a man very polite in his words, although at the time of the action he was highly violent and merciless against his enemies. After the cafeteria we went to the Agency to fulfill the routine, to see other colleagues, to stay on top of the progress of the mission. According to the new information obtained by the American Intelligence Agency, our plans were going very well, due to her extreme potential Sophia had immediate acceptance when applying for a position as a professional assassin in the criminal organization that had been terrorizing the world at the time.

Their fighting techniques, accompanied by perfect aim when using any weapon, was so excellent that it impressed even the most skeptical about the importance of women as combatants among them, since the East their space in any organization was still covered with prejudices.

He performed several tests with good results before fully conquering his space among his new companions, all criminals trained to kill anyone without hesitation. One of the most terrible was to kill an entire family in cold blood, executing one by one with shots to the head, from children to elders.

After being approved and accepted, he began to perform barbaric crimes in the name of the cause and PETROVIC, the leader of the organization, declared the number one enemy of all governments in the world, persecutor of religion, contrary to faith in a single, eternal, immortal and sovereign God.. For six months she worked together with Satan's son, even without knowing it.

He passed on to the Agency in New York all the necessary information to be able to identify each step of the enemy in real time, this made us get very close to each of his actions, knew his attack strategies and surprised them even before they acted. , but that raised suspicions.

— Commander, what's going on?

— Sorry, sir, what do you mean?

— I was informed that in the last attacks against our enemies we had a huge amount of casualties and we have not achieved the expected goal for the expansion of our conquests

— It's true, sir, but don't worry that we are doing everything possible to identify the reasons that are causing our enemies to surprise us

— It is good that this is resolved as soon as possible or we will have serious problems, check if there is no leakage of information in our environment, check the loyalty of each of our men from the smallest to the largest rank, especially those newcomers to us. our armies!

— No, sir, it will be done!

— Pass this order on to all of our military bases in all the countries in which we operate!

— Right!

PETROVIC was an intuitive man, he felt the threat from afar.

Because he was not an ordinary human being, he was guided directly by the gates of hell that guided him on a trail of destruction. After the emergence of drug trafficking and human lives, arms sales to opponents of world peace, the emergence of new criminal factions as well as wars increased considerably.

According to his orders, all new and old members of the criminal organization went through a fine-tooth comb, investigated everything in their lives, Sophia was in danger of having her disguise revealed and if that happened she would be tortured until she revealed important information about the Agency, placing the American Government on alert and all of us in great danger. At one point we received from our informant in Bosnia that the agent infiltrated the organization had already passed on to the CIA operations center installed there precise information…

Of where the base of PETROVIC operations was located and a scheme was already being drawn up for an attack where bombs would be dropped to destroy it. The biggest problem was to authorize Sophia to leave the mission and leave as soon as possible, because in the last three days they had lost contact with her, this made me apprehensive, something didn't seem to go very well with my friend. So I convinced my superiors that if within two more days she did not report it, I would rescue her myself.

My hope was that it would still be possible to rescue Sophia alive, since all that silence indicated that she would be unable to contact or possibly have been discovered which would result in torture or even her death. The forty-eight hours seemed to pass in slow motion, my distress was visible to everyone.

— Be calm, we need to hope

— Something's wrong, Richard, she was giving us news every day and suddenly disappearing from the radar without any clue as to her whereabouts?

— I agree with Luana, everything is really weird

— Anne is right, Sophia would have already given life if it were possible

— Congratulations, girls, now you worried me too!

— The worst thing is that tomorrow you will also go there and there will double our concerns!

— Do what, Mark, I need to go find out what happened to our friend

— If I could go with you

— We would all go, Richard! — Anne muttered

— Thank you very much for the support, but alone it will be easier to locate her

— Yes, that's what everyone at the Agency thinks

Night came and dawn ended on a Thursday morning, when the sun was still rising that beautiful day I was already on board an aircraft that would take me to our Intelligence center in Bosnia, where I would gather all the information necessary to locate , invade and release Sophia if she were still alive. However, it would not be easy to put this plan into practice.

After being fully informed I was taken by two agents to the indicated location where Sophia would possibly be imprisoned after it was revealed that she was an infiltrator in the PETROVIC organization, the area was mountainous and access was very restricted, in addition to being manned by a strong team security formed by the evil army.

Thanks to my enormous training while I was in the British Armed Forces it was not very difficult to climb the rocky wall that gave on the south side of the place. To go unnoticed by most of the guards, even though in some cases I had to eliminate some, entering the interior of the environment hostile and more guarded than the White House Forcing one of the men I took as a prisoner for a few seconds before executing him.

I was aware that a woman was being held in one of the many rooms there after being severely tortured for being an informant for the American government, I immediately understood how to treat the infiltrated agent.From the tip I was given.

It was even easier to locate the place where they would have taken her, after dominating several soldiers without having to fire a single shot, maintaining the necessary silence so as not to attract everyone's attention, I finally found her.

— Come on, Sophia, come on! — I gave the warning after knocking out the two men who watched the door

— Luana, what are you doing here?

— Come on, hurry up!

— Where are the others?

— They just sent me, but stop asking questions, because we have to get out of here!

I took the keys from the knocked out guard and opened his bonds, we ran off quickly looking for the nearest exit, along the way we ran into some of the men who were watching the place and engaged in a physical fight to avoid the use of firearms, because we would be denounced by the sound of the shots and easily dominated.

With admirable agility, even wounded by the torture suffered by the executioners who wanted at all costs to force her to reveal confidential data of the operation, Sophia faced these brutes with incredible ease, together we took them all down without much effort. However, there came a time when it was not possible to remain confidential.One of the soldiers saw us fleeing towards the wall where I climbed in an attempt to escape by going down the southern part of the place, so he fired several shots in our direction to prevent the escape.

This drew the attention of the others who came towards us as if it was an examination of angry bees with those who invade their territory

— Men, the prisoner is on the run, stop her!

— Quick, divide and surround the entire perimeter!

— They are going towards the wall!

As we ran, they fired and scattered all over the place in order to stop us, but a helicopter was already waiting for us nearby as planned, it was enough that we could get there on time.

But everything indicates that fate was fighting us together with that band of evil doers, because even defending us in every way we were not able to go much further and we were cornered before we even reached the exit that would take us to the rock wall where we would be a helicopter waiting for us.

The two automatic pistols with about twenty shots each emptied, leaving behind a balance of forty dead, we still took two machine guns from those who fell and eliminated another large number of bandits, but it was not enough to stop them completely , that way we were caught alive and taken into captivity.

There we were tied by the wrists to a chain attached to the ceiling of that half-dark room and beaten for several hours until PETROVIC arrived to ask us personally about the reasons why we were there, however it was not easy to convince us of this feat, we remained in silence embarrassing the cursed. Because of this, we took another beating that left our faces deformed, but still without any success.

Because we told them nothing about the reasons for the mission or what we really intended. Then the order was given for us to be executed, they took us to a certain place on the outside of the lair where the jackals hid. There they put us on our knees in front of two bandits who aimed their weapons at us, awaiting orders to eliminate us, however, in that very moment in a trance and a vision came to me at the worst moment of my life. In a matter of seconds I went and returned from the depths where I had a reunion with Satan who made me a proposal.

He proposed that I agree to return to his kingdom as his queen, return to live from the practice of evil as before I was rescued by Archangel Michael and if he agreed, he would deliver Sophia and me from certain death. I had to decide quickly, because we were going to be executed in a matter of seconds, so I didn't see any other alternative.

I said yes to the bastard who sent me back to the execution scene where we were both on our knees before our enemies with our two hands tied back, waiting for the inevitable shot. However, as promised, the DEMO acted in our defense by sending its powers to be free from death. Suddenly a crash was heard and as if it were a circle of fire engulfing both of us.

We were taken out of there in the blink of an eye and taken to the place where the aircraft was waiting for us, it was the opportunity to get out of that hell. But I couldn't let PETROVIC and his bloody army escape. So, after releasing the bonds that held me, the second part of the agreement I made with the DEMO was fulfilled, as we agreed that after freeing Sophia from the hands of the criminals, she would receive the powers of the Queen Evil back and destroy the wretched.

Satan very much wanted me to return to his world of darkness, but he knew that to do that I had to do evil. In this way he returned my powers and I was dressed in armored armor where no bullet would go through, a sharp sword appeared in my right hand and in the left a shield, beside me a legion of demons all with bows, arrows, spears and their devices that followed me wherever I went. In a leap we flew from the rocky mountain back into the den of wolves, fighting a real fight against our enemies who received the bullet, but nothing could stop us.

Frightened to see the crowd we were and how ineffective their weapons were against us, they tried in every way to find a way to stop us, but to no avail. Me and my army of demons beheaded each of the damned, their bodies fell to the ground as their heads rolled under our feet, a river of blood trickled down the aged floor as we advanced towards all their hiding places in the underground.

Of that purposely created maze to confuse potential attackers. The battle lasted only a few minutes for the speed with which we eliminated the opponents, in that period we destroyed everything that moved in front of us. Anyway, after our attempt against the evildoers was completed.

We were transported out of there in a millisecond and taken back to the extraction point where Sophia and the pilot were waiting for me. When I underwent the transformation, receiving back all my powers as Queen of Evil, granted by the DEMO because I agreed to return to serve him while I lived on earth and after that stage to return to his kingdom through my physical death, Sophia and the official were terrified of not understanding anything they saw.

Upon my return to the mountain accompanied by my spiritual army composed of hundreds of fallen Angels they froze once more and she passed out, falling at my feet in complete delirium while Roger, the pilot of the aircraft yellowed. I no longer looked the same, my physical features changed, I became taller, stronger, resplendent. My hair was long, however, and was held under a red helmet made of pure gold. My eyes burned like flaming torches, I dressed like a warrior from Medieval times, I had a reddish-colored garment on my body.

 Looking like impenetrable armor, golden bracelets on my wrists, in his right hand the sharp sword that cut up to the wind, in his left hand a shield made by the most powerful metal alloy on earth. That beautiful appearance remained in front of those who were looking at me in terror and it gradually faded, soon I returned to normal. Restored to what it was before, I counted on Roger's help to wake Sophia and leave.

During the entire trip back to the Agency she questioned me about the transformation, I was scared and at the same time impressed by what she saw happening to me. Roger also asked how something so supernatural could have happened, for both of them it was almost unbelievable.

— But what was that, Luana, what the hell happened to you? It seems that she became a goddess or something like that, surrounded by a legion of monsters that looked more like demons from hell!

— And that spectacular transformation? Wow, it was surprising, very scary!

— Guys, calm down, this story is very complicated to explain.

We will need time so that I can keep you up to date, as I find out about it myself in a very short time

— Are you by any chance a mystical being? A goddess? Where did you come from, do you know Hercules, Zeus, the queen of the Amazons?

— I know, you must be Wonder Woman, the one from the movies that came to help humanity against these damn criminals!

— Do you two want to please stop these silly speculations?

— How can you ask us to forget everything we saw happening to you right before our eyes? It is simply impossible!

— I fully agree with Sophia!

"Pay close attention to what I am going to tell you, because this is something very serious: Nobody, exactly nobody inside or outside the Agency can know anything about what happened today on that mountain, you know what measures they take if any agent shows any suspected characteristic of mental decline. If they say that at any given moment they saw me being transformed into any being full of power and that I destroyed our enemies with a legion of demons from hell, the two will be immediately removed from their duties until they are appointed as cured by psychologists. Please don't compromise your careers, keep what you saw only for yourself, understand?"

— Worse that you are absolutely right, I had forgotten that

— Okay, better to keep quiet, but don't think that we are going to give up that conversation where it will explain to us exactly what the hell happens to you!

— Okay, after we introduce ourselves at the Agency and give our reports we will go out for a beer there we talk, I will try to explain how things work

— That's it!

After reporting to our superiors a false escape from enemy territory, without going into details about what really happened, because in full agreement we agreed to tell the same version of the story, claiming that we placed explosives in various parts of the enemy's headquarters that after we left from there it caused the explosion that caused the destruction.

— And how was all this possible if you were on the run all the time after you located the agent

— Before locating it, we see a deposit full of very C-4 weaponry, after rescuing the agent, we joined in the purpose of spreading several explosives in the record time, we calculated the ideal time for the explosion to occur, giving us the necessary space so we could be out of the headquarters of the crime before detonation began

— Were they not pursued?

— As planned I managed to get in and out of the place without being seen by the rest of the enemy army, I used a silent weapon and self-defense to contain the enemies that might see me, so it was possible to rescue the agent without any major confrontation and exchange of shots

— Very well, Major, we are once again grateful for your excellent cooperation with our country, undoubtedly the British Agency's praise for it is deserved, your performance was impeccable!

— Thank you sir!

As soon as we left the Agency, we went straight to a bar nearby, a place frequented by good-natured people and talked for several hours, where Sophia vented her disappointments.

— What a bunch of ingrates, I fucking suffered in that sty and they only know how to recognize what she did, look at that!

— What an elbow pain!

— It will hurt you, Luana!

— Calm girls, we came here to have fun and to clarify that mystery poorly explained!

— How badly explained, she hasn't even started to solve the mystery

—You are wanting to understand something beyond human understanding

— Ah, now we are both stupid, unable to understand your explanations? So how about starting to tell us how it all happens?

— Okay, so let's go ...

— We're all ears, honey, you can start

— Actually, I don't know how to say precisely why everything I'm going to tell you from now on, I just know that since I was a little girl I realized I had something strange with me

— How so strange?

— Stay still, Sophia, let her talk!

— You bore!

— At ten years old she had the body of a girl of fifteen, at school she was the smartest girl in the class, she had dreams, nightmares ...

In them I found myself in strange places where I had never been before, I saw strange people, they seemed from ancient times, sometimes I had semi-awake visions, I heard voices ... But everything got worse some time ago after I was already working at the Agency, when I had a strange dream in that I was taken to a horrible, dark place and talked to the DEMO.

— Cruz creed, friend, did you talk to the devil?

— Face to face!

— You're kidding with us, aren't you?

— No, Roger, everything I'm telling you is the purest truth! I said it would be hard to believe my story

— Okay, sorry, continue

— Suddenly I found myself walking down a narrow corridor that widened with every meter walked by me, many monstrous beings passed to and fro without realizing my presence, it was as if they could not see or feel me. They dressed like soldiers, wore helmets, spears, wore warrior clothes, some wielded swords and shields From one second to the next I found myself walking in another setting where there was a large throne covered with gold and surrounded by flames of fire, seated on it a giant, monstrous being, wore a shining star on his head, dressed like a king, his face was like a pig, he had earrings on his ears, nose and neck big rings, his hands and feet were similar to of the frogs. His eyes burned like the hottest flames, his voice was like the sound of thunder, the earth shuddered when he spoke.

He realized that I was there and told me to come over, it was the demon who revealed details about my past life that I didn't even know existed, showed me as if it were in a movie everything I was and did in another existence, the evils, the abominations that led me to die and be condemned by God to live in darkness. It was due to so many bad things that I practiced for two centuries that the Creator threw me into darkness, this condition of sinfulness attracted the attention of Satan who fell in love with me, becoming my queen in the kingdom of evil

— Saint Mary, are you telling us that this reincarnation conversation is true? That he lived several existences before that and did horrible things to the point that his spirit was cast into the darkness where he became the wife of the Devil himself?

— Exactly, Roger that's right

— This can only be a joke, brought us here to make fun of our face, was it?

— I said you wouldn't believe it, Sophia!

— But who in their right mind will believe such nonsense, Luana, do you happen to think we are two suckers?

— Easy there, Sophia, we should give her a credit, after all we saw what we saw together, we cannot deny that everything was extremely magical and inexplicable!

— That's right, Roger, it was just some magic that this smart girl did to deceive us!

— And how to explain the destruction of the PETROVIC Headquarters?

— It must have been as she reported at the Agency, she must have put C-4 on the structures before we escaped!

— And the fact that you appear out of nowhere on the mountain? Can you explain the appearance of those horrible beings that made you pass out? Give it time, woman, you can't deny what we witness!

— Look here, save me from all this distrust, if you don't believe your problem!

— Wait a minute, Luana, I believe you, the questionable one here is Sophia!

— That's because I'm no fool to believe in a fairy tale!

— Pure envy, that's what!

— Well, then forget everything you saw and heard, even more!

In the days that followed my two friends held on as they could to not comment on all the mysterious events they witnessed during the last mission we carried out in Bosnia. The confirmation by the Intelligence that we had really destroyed one of the main bases of the terrorist organization also earned us much praise.

The media publicized the first defeat of PETROVIC and its allies as a great achievement for both the Eastern and Western world, the governments of all democratic countries celebrated the fall of part of the criminal empire that was growing day by day and causing terror wherever it went that would pass. After that, the bandit reinforced his army even more, increased surveillance, hired more criminals, was on alert to prevent him from being surprised again.

As the son of Satan in human form, he did not die when we invaded his base. In the same moment that we started to destroy everything and everyone in that den of cursed jackals he simply evaporated from there, going to another part of the country where he remained there in secret for a few days, devising what would be the next step to be taken. Then he went in spirit to the dark regions of the earth to have a dialogue with his father to clarify what had happened.

— How good to see you in its natural form, my son, what brings you here?

— It is to see you again in your kingdom my father, I came to get answers about recent events in the world of the living. I need you to explain to me why the Queen of evil joined in the purpose of thwarting my plans regarding the destruction of the human race, since this mission was entrusted to me by the Lord when he decided to send me to the surface of the earth, incarnating me as the man who I became today?

— There are many questions, my son, I see that your mind is troubled, confused and it is not for less. Everyone here in this kingdom knows how immense my passion for the Queen is, how good it is for me to have her by my side. Seeing her in trouble in the current human form that she possesses, I did not restrain myself from bringing her here in spirit to make a proposal. We agreed that if I gave her the necessary power to defeat her army, leaving there alive with her friends she would return to me after disincarnating.

— So you mean I lost all those brave men, had my main base of operations destroyed because of an idiotic whim that makes you weak in front of that woman?"

It seems that over the centuries the ancient father of demons is losing the power to lead the kingdom of darkness, I think the time has come to give up your place on the throne

— How dare you mention such folly before your king, asshole? Remove the words of offense you just uttered or I will be forced to remind you of the power of my evil!

Outraged, he rises from his throne and casts an enormous amount of lightning, fire and thunder on the demon whom he calls his son, casting him several meters away. His anger could not destroy a spirit, but certainly the pain felt by him was very real, causing him to evaporate from there and return to the surface. It was a cold winter night, when I was in my apartment in the pleasant company of my best friends.

Roger and Sophia, when suddenly an explosion was heard and right in front of us a circle of fire emerged from where came a glorious celestial being, holding a smoking sword in his right hand, his eyes were like flaming torches, his beauty resembled that of the gods, who spoke to us:

— Hail, chosen of the Most High, I come in the name of your God to warn you of the precipice you are about to fall due to your apostasy of faith in the Almighty!

His voice boomed in our ears like the sound of the loudest of thunder, the radiance of his glory was so strong that the three of us fell unconscious at his feet just after hearing his words.

However, outside the physical body it was possible for us to contemplate it in spirit, and continue to listen to what it said.

Sophia and Roger were finally able to see and understand how true my statements about my previous reincarnations were, living together with the Devil for two centuries.

The evils committed, the forgiveness I received, the pious life and the rejection of the Creator. For the angel that appeared there suddenly revealed to them my whole story, not only with the richness of details, but also transported us to the past, showing each scenario where I lived, what I practiced, both in evil and in kindness in the times when I reincarnated in this world as Mother Teresa, a pious nun who dedicated her entire existence to the poor.

After that time travel, he introduced himself as Seraphim Gabriel, messenger of God sent with the mission of alerting me to the risk of giving in to the whims of Satan and becoming his slave again, of the need to remember and understand that the rebuke of Lord as for the practice of idolatry in the previous life it was out of love.

That I should not remain revolted by his correction, but rather try to correct my mistakes so that after disincarnating I return to the heavenly mansions, receiving praise from him for my achievements and overcoming. In addition, it should help me to convince Sophia and Roger to believe in my revelations of the spirit world, we commented this after we awoke from the vision:

— My goodness, what the hell was that?

— Certainly a divine being, in view of his glorious appearance!

— No doubt, Roger, he was a heavenly messenger

— Holy shit, you weren't screwing with us when you told that amazing story of going to hell talking to the Devil or something!

— Of course not, Sophia, why would you do something like that?

— I don't know, to try to be the center of attention, after all it's what it's been doing since it was called by the Agency

— You're kidding, right? Since when do I need this?

— See, you are already feeling that!

— Do you two want to do the favor to stop this unfounded dispute? They are both beautiful, intelligent and the best agents I have met so far, so try to behave as such, right?

— Well, I think it's better!

— But explain there, Luana, how is this business of watching these apparitions, talking to angels and demons ... Can you remember your past lives?

— No, Roger, at least while I am awake, but during sleep I am taken to a certain spiritual plane where I can relive part of everything that I lived in other existences, then I add up each of the visions, understanding previous lives and assimilating who in fact I went, I did and how I got here in this new reincarnation

— And it happens very often, like every night?

— Almost always, when it is not through dreams I lie down, fall asleep and am transported in spirit to scenarios never seen before, there I find myself dressed as a warrior from medieval times between battles.

Confronting powerful, ferocious enemies, stepping on the blood of my opponents . Sometimes I find myself in the lowest parts of the earth in the kingdom of darkness, at other times in paradise, on a higher plane ... Things like that

— Just like we saw you up there on the mountain, all powerful?

— That's right, my friend, just like that

— All messed up the beast!

— Are you going to start teasing again, Sophia?

— Ah, screw it!

— Do you have any mastery over this gift that can manifest some extraordinary power right now so that we can contemplate it once again awake and in a spiritual trance as occurred in the last visions?

— I have no control over these events, they usually occur unexpectedly

— Too bad, I wanted to see you become the Queen of Evil again, but live without having to pass out

— Don't worry, my friend, everything happens in due time

— And in relation to what the angel said, what decision do you think to make?

— I did not know that I had been judged in the Divine Court, nor had I received the condemnation for worshiping idols during my previous incarnation, although in my delusions I had flashes of my stay in paradise, however, if it was so and I resented the divine rebuke I I wish to strip myself of that feeling.

I will certainly try to be at peace with God, but that will only happen if he helps me to destroy the evil empire on earth led by the son of Satan

— And how do you intend to do that, do you think about trying to negotiate with God? Since when does the Almighty make agreements with human beings?

— Now, Roger, he was the one who first sent an angel to me

— I agree with you, my friend, if he is bothered by his return to the kingdom of darkness and wants to prevent this from happening, because he knows the evil that will cause mankind, so he must attend to his claims!

— That's right, Sophia, for that reason I will negotiate with the Most High. If he agrees to send his army of angels to fight with me against this demon from hell, I will turn my back on the Demo, I will not return to his cursed kingdom, nor will I return to acting on earth as the Queen of evil

— Perfect, that's how you talk!

Two weeks passed after that conversation and during that period I remained in the expectation that the divine messenger would reappear so that I could present my proposal, but nothing happened. We were all asked to appear at the Intelligence Agency so that we could be informed of the recent news.

According to what the PETROVIC armies have continued to grow and advance in several other countries around the world despite the recent destruction of their main existing base in Bosnia, there was an urgent need for us to act secretly once again to dismantle their plans. The CIA had in mind to send Sophia and me again on a top-secret mission in France.

Where the domain of the terror army, as they came to be called, expanded rapidly and countless innocents would have lost their lives. We accepted the call promptly, immediately leaving for Paris with the purpose of acting against the enemy, there we were received by the local authorities, later forwarded to the French Intelligence Command.

As I did not know how to evoke both divine and demonic beings, I just had to wait until from one moment to the next to be taken in spirit again to the world of the dead or to receive the visit of God's envoy again. Sophia and I were properly informed about the enemies' actions and then we put the plan into action.

In the same way that Sophia acted to infiltrate the main PETROVIC headquarters in Bosnia in the same way we did to be accepted among those who served her there and in a short time we were already part of her second largest army, working side by side with hundreds criminals to conquer more territories.

In the likeness of a hurricane we saw those soldiers invade cities, spread out on the streets like ants, invading properties, killing innocents, raping women of all ages, setting fire to their homes, stealing their property, sacrificing their children, taking possession of the land they passed through. forcibly without being arrested.

But, for the mission to be successful, it was necessary that we pretend to be on their side and not on behalf of their victims, that way we were forced to collaborate with all that carnage from hell. After infiltrating, we passed on information to the CIA command base in Paris, they in turn reported everything to the Greater Command in New York City.

With the information obtained from the action of their two agents infiltrating the enemy army, the allies against the destructive domain of PETROVIC came to know the exact location of their main command posts, the strategies of attack against this or that target, avoiding possible surprise attacks.

From then on, whenever the evil army planned to dominate a province or even a small village in the cities of France, they were surprised by the strong resistance of the Allied combatants who joined forces to defeat them. Upon realizing these things, Satan's son was very angry, calling his generals to an emergency meeting.

— Gentlemen, we are being attacked again by our enemies and with many casualties, they know exactly where we are going to attack, without a doubt there is a leak of information, do we need to silence this informant as soon as possible?

— Do you believe that the same thing that happened at the Headquarters of Bosnia is being repeated?

— I never find anything, general, I am always absolutely sure. Those miserable CIA have infiltrated someone among our people and are receiving information about our attack plans.

— Very well, sir, so how should we act?

— Draw up a plan to locate this wretch as soon as possible, I want him alive to give him what he deserves!

— Yes sir, right now!

Despite being the son of the Damned, at least one of his favorites…

PETROVIC could not identify us, since we were under the protection of the greatest power of darkness that covered us from his demonic gaze. In this way we remain hidden from your spiritual radar and your generals long enough to provide our superiors with all the information necessary for a surprise attack with the Special Forces.

The allies fell like a real bee examination on top of the second headquarters of the son of Satan, destroying his base entirely, culminating in his army considered invincible. At the same time that several squads were turning that place into ashes in various other parts of the world, other allies were doing the same.

It so happens that, even without the combatants' knowledge, there was a mysterious force among them that fought alongside them, giving them the ability to achieve their goals of victory. This invisible power came from the lowest parts of the earth, legions of demons who fought together with each soldier in the fight against evil.

It was, in fact, Satan turning against his own chosen one to satisfy me in order that at the end of my current existence I would return to his kingdom and live with him as his Queen. However, in the end it was not part of my plans to return to the kingdom of darkness or be his wife again.

I spent several days thinking about the possibility of accepting the Most High's proposal to maintain my communion with him so that at the end of my existence I could rise and not descend into the darkness. It turns out that after all those victories against Maligno's son, he would be indebted to him, he would have bills to pay. It was then that one morning, when only Sophia and I were in a certain part of the enemy base.

After having eliminated several of them during the bloody battle started hours earlier by the invasion of our allies, I called upon Heavenly Father to send help so much to destroy the PETROVIC army like the demons. I know that my attitude seemed unfair, because they were fighting alongside and in favor of our men, however, that was extremely necessary, because if it did not happen that way I would be forced to return to hell, something that I did not even consider.

It was then that suddenly a flash appeared in the skies followed by lightning, lightning and thunder. Hundreds of thousands of angels came out of it, prepared to fight a real battle against the human beings and demons present there, that meant God's answer to my prayer. Sophia once again shivered at the base, froze like a green stick, couldn't even breathe properly, especially when she saw the demons among the soldiers.

— My God, Luana, look how much monster in the middle of our allies!

— Yes, they are fighting on our behalf, but they were invisible to human eyes

— Did they come from hell to help us?

— Actually they are here to make me leave alive from here at the behest of the Demo

— It's because?

— Simple, he hopes that at the end of my journey here on earth I will accept to return to his kingdom and become his Evil Queen again

— And these other angels who came down from above and fight against PETROVIC's men and demons?

— They are Archangels, sent by the Most High to fight both sides and not allow demons to emerge victorious, I am not indebted to Satan nor be forced to return to the darkness

— You are too messed up, my friend!

— Thank you for reminding me!

— And why does it not become that powerful again and enter the battle with the angels of God?

— Because that heroine is the Queen of Evil, you fool, if she evokes that she manifests herself in me, I am signing an alliance with the devil!

— Credo, now it's chipped!

— Calm down, let's get out of this!

— I just want to see how if we are surrounded by the enemy from all sides, have you noticed the number of them?

— Yes, there are many, but no match for the Archangels, in a little while there will not be even their ashes left!

We remained there hidden among the rubble of the old building where the headquarters of evil was housed, watching the defeat of PETROVIC's army. But to our surprise this time he did not run away from the battle as before, joining the demons who, seeing the arrival of the Archangels.

Stopped fighting alongside the allies and started to face the celestial beings. At that stage of the confrontation all his men belonging to his army of criminals were already dead, only demons and Archangels should continue to fight that battle…

Therefore, he enlisted his brothers from darkness against the children of God, starting a war between gods.

Fifth Chapter: Battle Between Gods

Endowed with immense power, the son of the Cursed One roared his voice as if it were a huge earthquake, summoning all the other demons to follow him in the confrontation against the children of God. Michael, the prince of the Archangels, raised his fiery sword and ordered his companions to start the greatest of all battles between the beings of light and darkness.

Many lightning, thunder and lightning could be seen while the angelic beings cut Satan's disciples in half, however, none of them were hit by them, quickly reducing PETROVIC's army that decided to go down to hell to request reinforcements from the Demo, leaving him aware of my betrayal when asking for divine help.

— I warned you that turning against me to defend that damn was not a good deal, now she brought the Archangels to destroy us!

— Silence! I do not give you the right to disapprove of my decisions. I am the leader in this realm and what I do or do not do is only in my interest, I must admit that I made a serious mistake, but I will fix it.

— And how do you intend to contain the Archangels' action against our armies?

— By sending our best demons to battle, if we cannot destroy them at least we will expel them from the battlefield.

Go down to the lower prisons right now and order them to free BELZEBU and his army, let them go up!

— But this decision is too dangerous, they can destroy all mortals on earth in a matter of hours!

— To expel these intruders I am capable of destroying the whole of humanity, do not discuss my orders, obey!

— Okay, as you wish

BELZEBU and his fallen angels are mentioned in the Holy Scriptures as being the most powerful beings of darkness, with powers even greater than that of Satan himself, that is why he keeps them chained in the deepest caves of the center of the earth, they will be the ones who will confront Christ in the War of Armageddon on his second coming into this world.

Freeing them meant bringing about the end of human life on earth, as they have the power to multiply, that is, in a matter of minutes those hundred powerful demons would become millions of them spreading across the planet. It happened that Demo only thought about revenge, he wanted to make me feel guilty about the Apocalypse.

When the hundred beings of darkness appeared in the middle of the battle, a great crash was heard, it seemed that the earth would split in half, everything shuddered under our feet, black clouds darkened the sky that was once lit by the intense rays of the sun, it was terrible to live everything that.

Sophia gave a cry of dread, I cannot deny that I also turned yellow, the other demons stopped fighting against the children of the Most High and stepped back to make room for BELZEBU and his soldiers.

Miguel together with his warriors remained ready for the fight, however they stopped the fight, waiting for what would happen from then on

— So you came again to challenge us, Miguel? Do you think that because you defeated Satan and his weak armies on another occasion, you could have the same result this time? Well know that you only won before because my brothers and I did not participate in that first battle, but here we are to confront them as equals. Do you consider yourself the most powerful of the Archangels? For I am the greatest of all demons in strength and power, I will destroy you and then all this weak humanity that your God created!

In saying these menacing words, he started towards Michael and his celestial warriors with the fury of a wild animal, they advanced determined to turn their opponents to dust and ashes, but they forgot that it is not for nothing that those angels are considered the private army of the Most High, his royal guard, the shield that protects his kingdom.

The instant that BELZEBU pronounced his words in a threatening tone, the prince of the Archangels transmitted in thought all his words to the Son of God, who witnessed and heard everything from his throne. Aware that the opponent's power was actually superior to that of his greatest representative, he personally went down to the battlefield.

Staying in hiding he incorporated into Michael, possessing his celestial body to fight the powerful adversary that could only be defeated by him, but only the Archangels could see him. While the angels that accompanied Michael faced the ninety-nine evil beings BELZEBU confronted the prince of the Archangels, but without knowing that in him Christ was endowed with the greatest power in the entire Universe.

And when crossing their swords flashed lightning everywhere, launching it a long distance from where they were fighting. Admired by the power that came out of the Archangel and repelled him that way BELZEBU could not understand what had happened, since he was much more powerful than the celestial being. The son of God had prevented him from seeing him as well as everyone else who was there, with the exception of the army of divine angels.

Unhappy with the humiliation, the demon rises and launches himself again against Miguel who with an exceptional movement again hit him with his sword again, throwing him a far greater distance than the previous one, humiliating him even more before his followers.

Realizing that their leader was taking a tremendous beating from the prince of the Archangels and that they were also unable to defeat the heavenly army, the other demons began to retreat from the battle, cowering before those they thought to defeat. Gradually they surrendered in the presence of the brave warriors of heaven, confirming the defeat of darkness.

Outraged by the whole situation, BELZEBU fought tirelessly against his opponent in the hope of winning him in the fight that lasted several hours, they were two extremely powerful beings crossing their swords that flashed with lightning and sparks of fire everywhere. Christ remained in Michael with the purpose of shaming Satan through him.

Sophia and I remained hidden behind the wreckage there, watching everything up close, the battle of the gods very impressed my friend who had never seen anything so fantastic before. After a long time of struggle between good and evil,

Light and darkness, the Son of the Most High finally defeated his opponent. BELZEBU fell to the ground defeated, destroyed and humiliated before his army, shaming those who followed him, believing him to be the greatest man. But there was still little that the Lord had done to that exalted demon, who spoke arrogantly against the prince of the Archangels, doubting his ability to defeat him.

In this way, Christ left Michael and without me realizing he took me, dwelt inside me, filling me with his glory and power. Suddenly a strong light enveloped me, I was suspended from the floor, a loud crash was heard, my clothes disappeared and in their place I found myself in different robes, a long sword appeared in my right hand.

We were amazed at what they saw both Sophia and the demons were surprised by what happened to me, I was transformed into a kind of medieval warrior, as in ancient times, ready for combat. BELZEBU remained standing for about a hundred meters, wielding his sword without understanding all that.

I was taken by the Lord who acted within me, dominating my thoughts, my mind, my eyes were torches of fire that burned continuously and when speaking the sound of my voice was similar to the sound of many thunders. Then the Son of the Almighty used my lips to address the failed demon.

"Do you try to shame the warriors of the Most High, demon?" For now you will be overcome by the sword of a woman who is the greatest shame for a warrior, whether human or not, you will be ridiculed before the eyes of those who follow you from hell and spend eternity trapped in the chains of darkness!

Upon hearing the words that came out of my mouth, but uttered by the Son of God, BELZEBU was very angry and advanced in my direction, pronouncing threats.

— For I will show you that I will not go through this shame nor accept inert to your threats!

The fight between the devil and the Queen of Light, as the divine being I was transformed was called, started and to the disappointment of the damned, the powerful Son of God who possessed me began to strike him with his flaming sword, throwing him him away each time he tried to hit him, thus fulfilling what he promised.

The battle waged by the two lasted for several hours until the sunset of that day, when the darkness of the night approached I raised my sword in an impulse made by the one who lived in me and the sun stopped where it was after rising ten degrees returning the light on end of that afternoon, so we could continue fighting our fight until the winner was determined.

We tirelessly continued to fight each other until BELZEBU acknowledged his defeat, falling to his knees before me, at the feet of a warrior woman, shaming himself and those who followed him from the darkness. After being defeated, he was chained together with his subjects and returned to the prisons of hell.

During all that time when the battle of the gods PETROVIC remained at a distance, waiting to see how that confrontation would end. As soon as his greatest ally was defeated, he fled from there and appeared before the king of darkness to inform him of the bad news.

— It did no good to free the demons from the prisons and send them to fight the Archangels, because they have achieved nothing against them! He didn't know how powerful that Archangel was, he defeated BELZEBU and his army of demons with the greatest of ease!

— Well, I know Miguel's strength and power, especially when Christ is in him!

— What do you mean, it's in it?

— Michael was created by the Most High to be the leader of the most powerful army in the entire universe, he was given the power to receive the person of the Son of God within his heavenly body, as a cosmic force, becoming one hundred percent stronger than it already is

— So here's the explanation of the defeat of our biggest demon army

— That's right, he went down without you being able to see him and joined Miguel in the fight against BELZEBU and his subjects, it was like that with me on the day I rebelled and decided to go up to the third sky, where the Most High reigns to take- his throne, however my thousands of Cherubim and I lost our powers, glory and radiance, we became darkness afterwards thrown from heaven to earth as if we were dung, something rejected by the gods, condemned to dwell in darkness for all eternity .

— But BELZEBU was not completely defeated by Miguel, during the duel of the two a woman resembled a goddess, dressed like a warrior, carrying in her right hand a long smoking sword that seemed to shatter him with each strike

— And where did it come from?

— I do not know, my lord, what I can tell you is that she was as strong and brave as Miguel

— So it is easy to deduce who she was, certainly it was the Queen, she asked for help to the heavens and the Archangels came, Christ descended on Michael to defeat BELZEBU, then he took possession of her to grant him sufficient powers to defeat and humiliate it. In this way it made my kingdom today ashamed, because the best of my demons fell at the feet of a damn woman

— Yes, that makes perfect sense

— Of course it does! Now we have to gather all of our advice, we need to find a way to redeem ourselves from such shame, now go and gather all my advisers and your other three brothers, we have a lot to do!

— OK, I will do it!

In my second incarnation I was the mother of all prostitutes known among mortals as POMBAGIRA, I had the specialty of inciting men and women to practice sexual immorality in all its aspects. Because of that, I was sentenced to be born on earth in a new existence, but again as a woman.

Heavenly Father's purpose was for me to repeat my life in a body similar to the previous one, however, doing good and not evil so that in this way I would be forgiven for so many evils practiced against humanity.

That was how I became a nun recognized worldwide as a holy woman, chaste, dedicated to social causes, defender of the poor. However, I committed the sin of idolatry by following Mary, the Catholic goddess, created by the human mind.

A fictional being who does not exist in heaven only in minds cauterized by the doctrine of Catholicism. It was my only big mistake, however, a huge offense against the Holy God of the entire Universe and that condemned me to a new reincarnation.

Finally, I was born in this world destined to fulfill my Karma, my luck, my destiny, as someone who, from an early age, would lose his family and be driven by destiny to the point where I arrived. Now, aware of these truths because they were revealed to me by Miguel before returning to paradise, I decided to take my place in the Universe and choose a side to follow

After the Son of God left me, he took from me all the powers I had during the confrontation with BELZEBU, but he showed me that I could rescue them if I wanted to, just agree to join the army of Archangels in the battle that would be fought. across the land from that day to end the bloody government of PETROVIC.

Freeing humanity from its yoke, bringing world peace again, then descending the lower regions of the earth and battling Satan within his own kingdom, humiliating him, weakening his power, freeing those captive souls who might decide to repent, taking captivity up high.

Of course, the idea of being able to become a totally powerful being, not like before, when I only became the Queen of Evil a few times and then I became a mortal again, but permanently. Of course, despite the frustration caused by my adventurous partner fearful of never seeing me or being together again, I decided to accept it. Sophia returned to the Agency, started to live her life in the same routine as always, gained great prestige in front of our superiors.

Won the highest position in the largest secret organization in the USA. He still won the heart of Roger with whom he married, but they never wanted to have children due to the risky life they led. About me? Well, I was taken for dead during the battle waged against PETROVIC and his criminal army, leaving my best friend the legacy of never giving up on an achievement, even if it means having to leave the scene many times. My body was never found, but it did not question the idea of having been eliminated.

After all, with so many explosions that occurred during combat it was thought that my body had been blown up without the slightest trace of my existence being found on the spot. While everyone was quietly following their routines, only Sophia knew about my important secret, where I was and what I was doing.

Now, transformed into the Queen of Light and not from evil, I joined Miguel together with his thousands of Archangels and we set out abroad to destroy PETROVIC's armies, wherever there was only one of his followers, we transformed him into dust and ashes. We acted in secret, in the invisible, without anyone being able to see us with the naked eye.

I was no longer a mortal being, but I suffered the translation of the flesh into the spirit without going through physical death, as happened with Enoch and the prophet Elias mentioned in the Scriptures. I became a demigod, a heroine, a jewel of God. After many struggles against the legions of evil that destroyed the lives of the innocent on earth, it was time to descend, to go to the depths of the earth for the final duel against Satan and his demons, they had come together, made plans.

Strengthened their defenses, looking forward to yet another battle where good and evil would take place in their last duel. Michael and his Archangels flapped their wings towards the kingdom of darkness.

I accompanied them astride the wings of the prince of God, we invaded the gates of hell, we went over their watchmen, we reduced their weak defenses to ashes, we visited every part of that accursed den, we removed iron gates, we melted their bronze locks, we freed many imprisoned souls who cried for freedom.

All by making sure of your total repentance and sincere desire to want the love of God, as determined by Christ. Satan enlisted his best demons and came to confront us, but to his disappointment we were more powerful, brave, better fighting each fight. That was the beginning of the end, where Archangels and demons would measure their strength, where only one of the two sides would win.

The And

Lightning Source UK Ltd.
Milton Keynes UK
UKRC010919271120
374043UK00011B/188